BKEJWANONG DBAAJMOWINAN

Stories of Where the Waters Divide

BKEJWANONG DBAAJMOWINAN

STORIES OF WHERE THE WATERS DIVIDE

Edited and translated by
MONTY McGAHEY II

Makwa Enewed | East Lansing, Michigan

♾ The paper used in this publication meets the minimum requirements
of ANSI/NISO Z39.48-1992 (R 1997) (Permanence of Paper).

Makwa Enewed
Michigan State University Press
East Lansing, Michigan 48823-5245

Library of Congress Cataloging-in-Publication Data is available
ISBN 978-1-938065-12-5 (paperback)
ISBN 978-1-938065-13-2 (PDF)

Book design by Charlie Sharp, Sharp Des!gns, East Lansing, Michigan
Cover design by Erin Kirk
Cover art courtesy of Nick Riley

Michigan State University Press is a member of the Green Press Initiative and
is committed to developing and encouraging ecologically responsible publishing practices. For more information about the Green Press Initiative and the
use of recycled paper in book publishing, please visit *www.greenpressinitiative.org*.

Visit Michigan State University Press at *www.msupress.org*

Contents

Mkadebineshii-kwe

Jennie Blackbird gii-dbaajma / Stories told by Jennie Blackbird

Bemgiizhgookwe

Joanne Day gii-dbaajma / Stories told by Joanne Day

Doopinibiikwe

Linda George gii-dbaajma / Stories told by Linda George

Noodin

Eric Isaac gii-dbaajma / Stories told by Eric Isaac

Naawkwe-giizhgo-kwe

Reta Sands gii-dbaajma / Stories told by Reta Sands

Mkoons
Ira White gii-dbaajmo / Stories told by Ira White Sr.

Kaangaadese
Edwin Taylor gii-dbaajma / Republished story told by Edwin Taylor

Preface

Boozhoo kina wiya, Ozaawaa Giizhgo Ginew ndizhinikaaz. Mzhiikenh ndoodem. Anishinaabe miinwaa Oneida ndaaw. Chippewas of the Thames ndibendaagoz. Monty McGahey II zhaagnaashiiwnikaazayaanh.[1] I am a second-language speaker and have become proficient in speaking Anishinaabemowin as an adult. Around 2007, I started my journey to reclaim my language by learning it from a variety of teachers and resources. The ability to speak my language and converse with fluent speakers has strengthened my identity as Anishinaabe.

There are no first-language speakers of Anishinaabemowin from my own community of Chippewas of the Thames First Nation located in Southwestern, Ontario. Our community hasn't had a fluent member living on our territory since the 1980s. Mount Elgin Indian Residential School was located within our community and was opened in 1841.[2] The detrimental impacts of the nearly one hundred years that it was in operation are still felt in the community. It is my understanding that the school is a major contributing factor to the loss of language in Chippewa of the Thames First Nation.

Since I do not have access to fluent speakers who are originally from my community, I have developed relationships with many fluent speakers in Bkejwanong, also known as Walpole Island. Bkejwanong is just over an hour drive from my community and is located along the boundary that is known as the Canada and United States border along the St. Clair River in Southwestern Ontario, Canada. It's the closest community to mine that has fluent first-language speakers. There are very few fluent speakers left in Southwestern Ontario within Anishinaabe communities. The youngest fluent speaker from Bkejwanong is around seventy years old. There is an urgent need to document Anishinaabemowin from the aging population of speakers in these communities. Since I have developed working relationships with fluent speakers from Bkejwanong, I decided that producing a bilingual book would be one way to help document and preserve the regional dialect.

As I've been learning how to speak Anishinaabemowin, I've come across many helpful resources. A few of these resources are bilingual books containing stories in Anishinaabemowin along with the English translations.[3] These stories are transcribed from oral accounts of fluent speakers. I have found that Anishinaabemowin stories that are transcribed from recordings of fluent speakers capture the language more accurately and authentically than those that are written as Anishinaabemowin translations from English versions.

For this project, I recorded six fluent speakers from Bkejwanong telling various stories that they heard growing up as well as their own stories from their personal experiences. The process of completing the book took longer than originally planned. First, I transcribed each story in Anishinaabemowin with the common writing system used today, which was created by Charles Fiero and is also called the "double-vowel" writing system (see "Ojibwe: Fiero Spelling System"). I then tried to translate as much as I could with my own knowledge of Anishinaabemowin and with the use of language resources. Finally, I went back to each fluent speaker for their own translations of the stories. The transcription process helped heighten my understanding of the language, as I was able to repeatedly and carefully listen to the recordings of the speakers while also having to write down what they said. At the request of one elder, I've also included two stories that have been previously published in another book.

In order to faithfully depict local pronunciation, I used reputable dictionaries and made modifications when needed. I tried to spell words in accordance with the *Eastern Ojibwa-Chippewa-Ottawa Dictionary* and the *Nishnaabemwin Online Dictionary* as closely as possible. These two dictionaries are the most widely used among teachers and learners of what is mainly called Eastern Ojibwe, which covers central and southern Ontario and Michigan.

Yet there are still some differences in spelling between these two resources. Perhaps these differences result from the Fiero writing system, which follows the sounds speakers make but does not implement a standardized way of spelling. Therefore, localized or regional differences in pronunciation impact how spelling is represented in different dictionaries. An example of this is the word "Anishinaabemowin" itself. There are now resources that spell the same word "Nishnaabemwin." It has the same meaning but with some vowel sounds unspoken. The spelling of this word depicts the way a speaker from Bkejwanong and some other communities might pronounce it. The shortening of the words or the dropping of vowels is associated with what some scholars say is the

Odawa dialect. This dialect is said to be spoken in southern and central Ontario and central and southern Michigan. It is distinct from the dialects spoken in other areas because the words spoken are shortened due to the dropping of vowels, which is called syncopation.

However, if you ask a fluent speaker anywhere, especially Bkejwanong, they would say they speak Ojibwe or Anishinaabemowin. I have not yet heard a speaker explicitly say they speak strictly Odawa. Since the early 1800s there. has been a large contingent of Boodwe'aadmii (Potawatomi) people that migrated into Canada and into many Indigenous communities, including Bkejwanong, which may have had an influence on the way of speaking Anishinaabemowin. As with other communities in southwestern Ontario and Michigan, Boodwe'aadmii, Odawa, and Ojibwe were all living together and speaking to each other before the 1800s. Thus, there is the challenge of maintaining consistent spellings of Anishinaabemowin words for modern learners since there are variations of pronunciation between regions and even between speakers within the same community.

Differences in pronunciation are important to record, but they can pose challenges for learners. Second-language learners, like myself, like things such as spelling and grammar to be consistent because predictability helps with grasping any new language. However, the complex nature of language often does not accommodate this preference. In addition to the omission of certain vowels, some of the words spoken by the speakers for this book change depending on when the word is said in the sentence and/or how a speaker pronounces it. For example, the pre-verb "gchi" modifies a word to mean bigger or greater (gchi-miigwech means "big thank you" or "thank you very much"). At times speakers pronounce the word with a "g" (gchi-) and at others without it (chi-). However, in both dictionaries mentioned earlier, "gchi-" is always written. I decided to spell the words both ways (with gchi- and chi-) in order to follow how it is spoken by the speaker in a particular sentence. Another example is a word that is used to mean "again" or "and" and is glossed by both dictionaries as "miinwaa." Most of the speakers I recorded pronounce it as "miin'aa," leaving out the sound of the "w." Moreover, there are other instances throughout the book where I had to make a decision about whether to write words as they are spelled in dictionaries or how they are pronounced by a speaker while still following the Fiero writing system. Generally, I followed the dictionaries, but I used my own discretion in certain instances and slightly changed the spelling of particular words to more closely follow how the fluent speaker had said it.

In addition, throughout the book you will see words or phrases with curly brackets { } around them. This shows that another speaker other than the main person telling the story was adding a comment. You will also see square brackets [ ] around words or phrases in the English translations. These brackets indicate a speaker's clarification or explanation of what they meant in particular parts of their story.

One of the most interesting things about learning Anishinaabemowin is the use of discourse markers. Discourse markers are the short sounds uttered between words. *Sa, go, dash, gsha,* and *mii* are some examples that can also be used in combinations such as *sa go, dash go, wii, gii naa, mii sa.* Speakers use these throughout their natural speech yet I've found that when stories are translated into Anishinaabemowin from English they are missing. One of the main reasons why I wanted to transcribe recorded stories from fluent speakers is to document the usage of discourse markers in order to better understand and to speak the language like fluent speakers. There seems to be an almost subconscious usage of these, as most fluent speakers I've talked to cannot explain the meaning of these discourse markers. This not by any means invalidating their mastery of speaking Anishinaabemowin. Even among linguists, discourse markers are hard to define. In the book *Ojibwe Discourse Markers* by Brendan Fairbanks, he does a tremendous job in explaining many of those that are used among fluent speakers in Minnesota and Wisconsin. As with the *shortening of words* mentioned above, discourse markers also become shortened. Some examples are *sa go naa* to *skonaa, mii dash* to *mii-sh,* and *dash wii go* to *shwii go.* In this book, I made the decision to write the shortened version of these—for example, *skonaa* if that's how the speakers said it—rather than writing it as *sa go naa.* There are other cases of this throughout the text. For learners, discourse markers will be a continuous learning curve even for intermediate and advanced speakers.

It is my hope that second-language speakers of Anishinaabemowin from not only Southwestern Ontario but also from other communities across Turtle Island (North America) can use this resource to assist them with their own learning and aid them in becoming proficient speakers. Moreover, I intend for this resource to be useful for preserving the language for the next generation of Anishinaabemowin speakers.

NOTES

1. Introduction translation: Hello everyone. My name is Ozaawaa Giizhgo Ginew. I'm turtle clan. I am Anishinaabe and Oneida. I belong to Chippewas of the Thames First Nation. My English name is Monty McGahey II.

2. "Mt. Elgin Industrial Institute—Indian Residential School History," Chippewas of the Thames First Nation, https://www.cottfn.com/mt-elgin-industrial-institute-indian-residential-school/.

3. See Howard Webkamigad, *Ottawa Stories from the Springs: Anishinaabe dibaadjimowinan wodi gaa binjibaamigak wodi mookodjiwong e zhinikaadek* (East Lansing: Michigan State University Press, 2015); Brian McInnes, *Sounding Thunder: The Stories of Francis Pegahmagabow* (East Lansing: Michigan State University Press, 2016); Leonard Bloomfield, *Weshki-Bmaadzijig Ji-noondmowaad: Stories of Andrew Medler* (London, ON: Centre for Research and Teaching of Canadian Native Languages, 1998); Anton Treuer, *Living Our Language: Ojibwe Tales and Oral Histories* (Saint Paul: Minnesota Historical Society Press, 2001); Ojibwe Cultural Foundation, *Gechi-piitzijig Dbaajmowag: The Stories of Our Elders: A Compilation of Ojibwe Stories, with English Translations* (M'Chigeeng: Ojibwe Cultural Foundation, 2011); and Maude Kegg, *Portage Lake: Memories of an Ojibwe Childhood*, ed. by John D Nichols (Minneapolis: University of Minnesota Press, 1993).

ACKNOWLEDGMENTS

This book would not have been possible without the support and participation of the fluent speakers: Doopinibiikwe, Linda George; Bemgiizhgookwe, Joanne Day; Naawkwegiizhgokwe, Reta Sands; Mkoons, Ira White Sr.; Noodin, Eric Isaac; and Mkadebineshii-kwe, Jennie Blackbird. Brandee Ermatinger and Mko-giizoons, Tiffany Myers, were also instrumental in helping get this book together. The Ontario Arts Council made this possible through the Indigenous Culture Fund. A special miigwech goes to Linda George, who connected me with other fluent speakers in Bkejwanong, and Jennie Blackbird, who helped me with the finishing touches in the translations of the stories and has also helped me tremendously in my personal language learning journey. The royalties of this book will go directly to the Anishinaabe Language Advisory Group in Bkejwanong to help with their language initiatives.

Ojibwe: Fiero Spelling System

The most common spelling system used among Anishinaabemowin teachers and learners is called Fiero or double-vowel spelling system. Using the Roman alphabet, all of the vowel and consonant sounds are consistent throughout. To be clear, there is not one correct way to spell a word. The sound system follows the speaker's way of speaking. For example, the Anishinaabemowin word for "song" can be "nagamowin" or "ngamwin."

FIERO SPELLING CHART

VOWELS	ENGLISH SOUND	OJIBWE SPELLING
a	nut or uncle	miikan (road)
e	set or effect	miigwech (thank you)
i	pin or it	piniig
o	look or took	bmose
aa	taught or saw	baamaapii
ii	beet or feet	miijim
oo	row or boat	goon

OTHER SOUNDS

aaw: This sounds like "how," as in "ahaaw" (OK).

aw/ow: This sounds like "oh," as in "ow" (that person/animate object).

ay: This sounds like "ice" or "bike," as in "nday" (my dog).

iw: This sounds like "few," as in "niw" (those objects).

Glottal stop: This is punctuation used to indicate a break in the word, as in "aate'aan" (extinguishing a fire).

n: This is a nasal sound, like speaking with your nose plugged. As an ending, it is written "nh" as in "giishenh" (little bit). In the middle of the word, use letter "n" as in "jaanzh" (nose).

RESOURCES

White, Lena. *Ojibway Reference Booklet*. Unpublished, 1988, Lakehead University, Thunder Bay, ON.

Walpole Island Language Centre. *Miijim Mazinigan*. Walpole Island (Bkejwanong), ON: Walpole Island Language Centre, 1976.

BKEJWANONG DBAAJMOWINAN

Stories of Where the Waters Divide

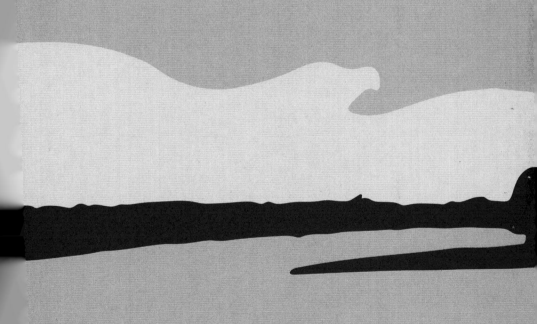

Mkadebineshii-kwe

Jennie Blackbird gii-dbaajma / Stories told by Jennie Blackbird

GAA-ZHICHGEWAAD

1   Oh na'aa, Jennie Blackbird genii ndizhinikaaz.

2   Mii go naa genii gii-bi-kognigooyaanh maampii mnishe'ing, Walpole Island.

3   Pii gii-gaashiiyaanh mii go eta gaa-noondmaanh maanda Anishinaabemowin.

4   Gaawiin zhaagnaashiimwin ngii-noondziin gii-binoojiinwiyaang.

5   Mii dash iw wenjda gwa gii-gyakwan iw pii.

6   Kina ge go naa gii-giiwsewag miinwaa ge giigoonkewag miin'aa ge go naa wenjda go kina go gegoo gii-biinaabminaagod.

7   Maanda ge nesewin wenda go gii-biinaagod.

8   Miin'aa ge iw ni'ii nanda ziibiinsan, creeks, wenjda go gii-biinaagmisinoon.

9   Miin'aa ge ni'ii chi-ziibi, St. Clair River, wenjda gwa gii-biinaagmi.

10   Mii iw gaa-zhiwebak iw gii-binoojiinwiyaanh genii.

11   Mii dash iw kina gegnaa gii-gtigewag.

12   Kina go ni'ii bezhgoogzhii ge go ngii-yaawaanaa, gii-gtigewag.

WHAT THEY DID

1   Oh, ah, Jennie Blackbird is my name.

2   This island is where I was born and raised, Walpole Island.

3   When I was small, all I heard was Anishinaabemowin.

4   I never heard English when we were children.

5   It was really awesome at that time.

6   All they did was hunt and fish, and everything was clean [natural].

7   The air was clean [no pollution].

8   Even the swamps and the creeks were clear and clean.

9   Even St. Clair River was clean.

10 That's how it was like when I was a child.

11 So everyone planted gardens.

12 We all had horses; they gardened.

13   Wenjda shko naa ngii-mno-yaami.

14   Miin'aa dash gonda gaa-giiwsejig chi-gamiing wodi kina giiwsewag.

15   Zhashkoonh miin'aa waawaashkesh miin'aa zhiishiibag miin'aa ge kagwag miinwaa oodi ni'ii chi-gamiing.

16   Na'aa ninaabeba gii-biinaan na'aa piniin, wild potatoes wodi, they grew, wodi chi-gamiing.

17   Miin'aa jiisenyan, jiisensan miin'aa na'aa, onions, kina go nanda, they were wild, ninda.

18   Waawaach go naa ni'ii niibiishaaboo. Ni'ii niibiish iw. Gii-aabjitoonaawaa.

19   Mii dash iw noongwa, wenjda go naa zanagad noongwa iw ezhiwebak nji go maaba ewaabshkiiwed.

20   Miin'aa ge bemaadzijig gii-bmosewag.

21   Wenjda go gii-mna-bmaadziwag and um miinwaa mii go pane gaa-piitnakiiwaad.

22   Mii go ni-dibikak, mii go geniinwi gii-nbaayaang, ngii-yekzimi wenjda shko ge go naa ngii-mna-mbaami gii-gtaamgo-nakiiyaang.

23   Gonda dash biiweziimag niibna ngii-dchimi.

24   Maaba dash na'aa. Shirley miin'aa Maanii miin'aa Helena miin'aa niin ngii-ziigwebnigoomi widi ni'ii residential school.

25   Gonda dash aanind, na'aa ndawemaa Agnes*, miin'aa Harriett. Oodi gewiinwaa training school gii-zhinaazhkaajgaazawag.

13   We had a good life.

14   And these hunters would all go hunting across the lake [United States].

15   The hunters hunted muskrat and deer and ducks and geese over there across the lake.

16   My late husband use to bring home wild potatoes from the marsh.

17   And wild carrots, and um, onions, every one of these, they were wild, these ones.

18   Even tea, these were the leaves they used for tea.

19   We're living in perilous times because of the white man.

20   And all they did was walk.

21   They had a healthy life, and um, they continuously worked.

22   And at night, when we went to bed, we always slept well because we worked hard.

23   There were a lot of us in my family.

24   This one [person] um. Shirley and Mary and Helena and I, we got dropped of over there at the residential school.

25   And as for some of them, my older brother Junior [speaker corrected name in translation] and older sister, Harriett, they were sent to a training school.

26 Miin'aa bezhig na'aa niijkiwem Joey, gewii widi foster home.

27 Mii dash giw aanind na'aa, nwiijkiwemag, Junior* miin'aa na'aa Frank mii go eta giw gaa-yaajig.

28 Gii-shkonjgaazawag giw. Nshiimenh. Nshiimenyag.

29 And ah. Mii dash iw, kina go ngii-nishnaabemmi. Wenjda gwa gii-ntaa-nishnaabemwag giw.

30 Mii go eta gaa-noondamaanh iw anishinaabemwin.

31 Mii dash iw, maaba bezhig na'aa, Agnes gii-zhinkaazo. Wenjda go gii-mshkonakii ow.

32 Wenjda go gii-gtaamgozi. Gii-gtaamgwatoo. Maaba Agnes ezhinkaazad.

33 Wenjda go gii-gtaamgwan ... she worked like a horse.

34 Mii go maanda biigbidoon maanda biindig. Mii go neyaaptood iw. She could tear a house apart.

35 Mii go iw. Mii iw gaa-piitnokiid.

26   And my brother Joey was sent to a foster home.

27   And the other ones, my brothers, Larry [speaker corrected name in translation] and Frank, were the only ones that stayed home.

28   They were left behind. My younger sibling. My younger siblings.

29   And ah, and then we all spoke Anishinaabemowin. They spoke it really well.

30   That's all I heard was Anishinaabemowin.

31   And this other one who was called Agnes [my younger sister]. She was a really hard worker.

32   She was a strong spirited woman. This one called Agnes.

33   She was really… she worked like a horse.

34   She would tear the house apart inside. Then she'd put it all back together. She could tear a house apart.

35   That's it. That's how hard she worked.

SHIRLEY ROSE ZHINKAAZA

1   Maanda ge pii gaa-ndaadzid. Ge giikaandimi.

2   Aanii da giinaa uncle ge-kidpa wiya? Uncle.

3   Mii gnabaj iw, 'zhishenh?' Gii-giikaandimi.

4   Aanii da giinaa maanda. "Shirley Rose nindawendmaanh wii-
    zhinikaazad maaba," ndinaa.

5   Aanii da giinaa gaa-kidad? "Mii iw nendawendmaanh genii to be her
    name," gii-kida.

6   Rosemary. Yeah, Rosemary, gii-ndawenmaan maaba wii-zhinikaazad.

7   "Onh," mii dash gii-gchi-mwiyaanh.

8   "Onh, mama! Gaawii iw!"

9   'Shirley Rose' maaba ndi-ndawenmaa maaba zhinkaazad.

10 Ngii-bkinaage. Mii dash iw 'Shirley Rose' noongwa zhinkaaza.

11 Mii shii ge ow.

HER NAME IS SHIRLEY ROSE

1   This one time, when she [my sister] was born. We [my uncle and I] argued.

2   Oh, how does someone say uncle? Uncle.

3   Maybe it's "zhishenh"? We argued with one another.

4   Oh, what did I say? "I want her to be named Shirley Rose," I said to him.

5   What did he say again? "That's what I want to be her name," he said.

6   Rosemary. Yeah, Rosemary, he wanted her to be named that.

7   "Oh." And then I started crying.

8   "Oh, mama! Not that one!"

9   I want her to be named Shirley Rose.

10   I won. So today her name is Shirley Rose.

11   Yeah, that's her [now, Shirley Rose].

GII-BI-GZHAADAAWSAD NSHIIMENH

1 Miin'aa ge maaba ngoding gii-bi-gzhaadaawsa wodi endaayaanh.

2 Mii dash ow ge gii-gaachii iw na'aa Babe, Shirley Rose.

3 Wodi dash, oodi ni'ii ziibiing ngii-wo-gziibiignaanan ni'ii aanziiyaanan.

4 Pii dash gaa-bi-bskaabiiyaanh "Aapiish naa wa na'aa ndabiibiinsim?" ndinaa maaba. "Yooo!" kida.

5 Oooh geget ngii-ndowaabmaanaa naabemba. Ooh wenjda go gii-zegzi.

6 Mii dash maaba oodi miikanaang gii-zhaad gii-waabdang niw wodi toward the main drag oodi gii-zhi-bmose ow.

7 Mii gwa eta aanziiyaan. Gii-bmikwe.

8 Maaba gaa-gzhaadaawsad.

9 Other speaker: {Gaa gii-waabmaasii oodi zhaanid?}

10 Gaa, well na'aa ni'ii aanind gii-gzhaa'aan.

11 {And I was ironing too at the same time.}

12 {Gii-gjibigoon.}

13 {Enh, gii-gjibwe}

WHEN MY LITTLE SISTER BABYSAT

1   And this one time she came to babysit at my house.

2   And she was small, "Babe," Shirley Rose.

3   I was washing diapers over there at the river.

4   Then when I came back, I asked her, "Where's my baby?" And she says, "Yooo!"

5   We went looking for her. My husband too. We were petrified.

6   Then my husband went out to the road and went walking toward the main drag.

7   With only a diaper. She left footprints.

8   She [Shirley] was the babysitter.

9   Other speaker: {You didn't see her go over there?}

10 She didn't see her because she watched her sometimes.

11 {And I was ironing too at the same time.}

12 {She ran away from her.}

13 {Yeah, she ran away.}

14   Mii dash iw gii-waabdang iw gii-bmikwed ow na'aa, {Babe}, niijaanis, ooh gwet … gii-gwaansikmiid.

15   {Gwetaanbiza.} Gaa ge aapji daabaanag gii-yaasiiwag.

16   Mii sa geniin gaa-zhiwebziyaang iw.

14   She went looking, and she saw the tracks made by {Babe}, my child. Oh, … she took off really fast.

15   {She drove fast.} There were hardly any cars in them days.

16   That's what happened to us.

GDABMIWDOONAAWAA MAANDA NISHNAABEMWIN

1 Mii dash iw noongwa genii ezhi-maamiikwendmaanh noongwa maanda giinwaa enankiiyeg. Brandee, Monty, miin'aa na'aa, Betsy (Kechego).

2 Giinwaa bmiwdooyeg maanda. Maanda ni'ii, nbwaakaawin edzhindamaang, ji-bmiwdooyeg maanda.

3 Giinwaa. Warriors, Miigaazo-nini aawi, Miigaazo-niniikwe maaba, miinwaa na'aa Betsy. Gewii go ow Miigaazo-niniikwe gewii aawi ow.

4 Maanda ni'ii nbwaakaawin edzhindamaang ji-bmiwdooyeg maanda, giinwaa.

5 Wenjda shko ggchi-piitenminim iw giinwaa enankiiyeg.

6 Noongom maanda pii, miinwaa aapji go znagad maanda ni'ii nishnaabemwin gonda bemaadzijig.

7 Mii dash giinwaa gdabmiwdoonaawaa maanda sa ni'ii nishnaabemwin.

8 Giinwaa pii maajaayaang.

9 Giinwaa gdamiiyaawshkaagon maanda wii-bmiwdooyeg maanda anishinaabemwin.

10 Niin shko naa genii debnaak go mna-bmaadziyaanh, miin'aa weweni naanaagdawendmaanh ezhi-gookshki'ewziyaanh gwii-naadmoonim.

YOU ALL ARE CARRYING THIS LANGUAGE

1   I'm so happy today that you all are doing this [recording fluent speakers]. Brandee, Monty, and um Betsy (Kechego).

2   You all will be carrying this. This wisdom that we're talking about, you all will carry it.

3   You all. Warriors, he's a warrior and she's a warrior, and Betsy. She's also a warrior.

4   This what you're carrying. You're carrying wisdom. You're going to run ahead with this knowledge.

5   Really, I think very highly of the work you all are involved in today.

6   Nowadays this Anishinaabemowin is hard for the young people.

7   And so you're the ones who are carrying the language.

8   You all will when we're gone.

9   It'll be up to you to carry the language.

10   As for me, just as long as I'm healthy and have a clear mind, I will endeavor to do my best. I'm going to help you.

11 Maanda ni'ii Anishinaabemwin ezhi-gchi-piitendaagwok maanda
Gzhe-mnidoo gaa-miingooziying.

12 Wenjda gwa mnataagod maanda gaa ge ni'ii mji-giizhwewin
yaasinoo maa maanda ni'ii, maanda ni'ii. Enh, nwewin.

13 Mii dash iw aapji genii ngchi-nendam naadmaageyaanh maanda.

14 Gzhe-mnidoo gaa-zhi-zhawenmigying miinwaa naadmaagying gaa
ge wiikaa mnikwewin gii-yaasinoo maampii Anishinaabeg.

15 Mii go gonda Zhaagnaashag gaa-bi-bnaajchigejig.

16 Mii dash iw geniinwi ezhi-ko-gshki'ewziyaang maaba enmadbid
Shirley zhinkaaza, oodi ge Linda, Doopinibiikwe gwii-naadmaagoom
maanda ni'ii anishinaabemwin.

17 Wenjda-sh go gchi-piitendam giinwaa, maanda noongwa enankiiyeg.

11   This language is sacred. This God-given language that was given to us.

12   It sounds powerful. And there's no swear words in the sounds.

13   Also, I'm so proud and happy to help out with this.

14   How God blessed us and helped us. There was never alcohol in North America.

15   The white people were the ones that ruined everything.

16   And so, this is how far we, the one sitting here, Shirley [Ermatinger)] is her name, over there, Linda, Doopinibiikwe, are endeavoring to help you all with this language.

17   And I think highly of the work you're doing now.

Bemgiizhgookwe

Joanne Day gii-dbaajma / Stories told by Joanne Day

GII-WAABMAAD NOOS PA'IINSAN

1   Boozhoo, Joanne Day ndizhinikaaz. Bemgiizhgookwe Anishinaabewinikaazayaanh.

2   Miinwaa maampii bi-njibaa, ni'ii Bkejwanong.

3   Mii maa endaayaanh.

4   Giishenh go eta gegoo nii-dbaajdaan, gegoo go naa gaa-bi-zhi-gkendmaanh genii zhaazhi go naa jibwaa wiidgeyaanh gegnaa.

5   Gojiing go naa gii-bbaa-yiyaayaanh.

6   Mii-sh maanda nii-dbaajmaa gonda yaa'aak … pa'iinsag gii-zhinkaazawag.

7   And miinwaa na'aa, noos ko pane gii-oo-nankii wodi 'iing nookming. Pane gii-dnakmigzi.

8   Giishkboojged miinwaa daawed niwi ni'iin, mtigoon.

9   And um, mii gewii gaa-nankiid iw wii-gshkitood zhoonyaa. Zhoonyaans.

10   Gii-noojgaaza go naa ko wii-oo-giishkboojged oodi miin'aa gii-giishnadmowind niwi ni'iin mtigoon.

11   Mii-sh, ngoding oodi zhaad.

WHEN MY DAD SAW LITTLE PEOPLE

1   Hello, my name's Joanne Day. I'm Bemgiizhgookwe when I'm called by my Anishinaabe name.

2   And I'm from here. Bkejwanong [Walpole Island].

3   That's where I live.

4   I'm just going to talk a little about something that I know about that happened long time ago before I was even married.

5   I would be around outside.

6   So I'm going to talk about those ones ... little people, they're called.

7   And my dad always use to be back in the bush working. Always working.

8   He cut and traded those trees.

9   And um, that's what he use to do to make money. It was a little bit of money.

10   They use to hire him to go and cut wood and sell it to people.

11   Then, one time, when he went over there.

12   Ngoding go naa bi-giiwed. Oh gii-yaa go naa ko gii-ni-dbikad go naa
      ko gii-bi-giiwed.

13   Oh megwaa go naa ko bi-njiwse oodi. Bi-njibaad nookming.

14   Mii-sh go naa maaba ngashi mii iw gaa-naad "gesnaa go gegii wodi
      gbeyiing bbaa-yaa. Mii go naa dbikak maa bi-biindgeyin."

15   Nishkaadzi ko.

16   Mii dash ngoding bi-giiwed maa naakshig go naa iw. Mii dash
      wiisiniyaang.

17   Mii dash ekidad iw. "Oh ngii-maakmiikwaab sa niin wi noongwa,"
      kida.

18   "Nookming?" dinaan shko gewii nimaamaa. "Enh." "Wenesh oodi
      gaa-waabndaman?" dinaan.

19   Mii dash niw wiyan binoojiinyan gii-waabmaan.

20   Na'aa kwezensag bbaambatoowaad, gaawii go besho. Gii-
      debaabmaan oodi nikeyaa waasa nwanj.

21   "Bbaambatoo. Oooh, gchi-damnawag," dinaan.

22   "Mii-sh go naa gii-nookshkaayaanh maa enokiiyaanh," kida.

23   "Mii go naa gii-naaniibwiyaanh maa gnawaabmagwaa. Oooh wenda
      gwa gnaajwani ni'ii ebiiskamwaajin," kida. "Oh ge go gwiiwzens.
      Wenda go gewii weweni go gii-zhinaagzi," kida.

24   "Maandaawnaagoziwag shko naa," *ya know*, "bkaan go naa nikeyaa
      gii-nikoniyewag."

12 One time he came home. He use to stay there when it was dark. That is when he came home at night.

13 He use to come walking from over there. When he came from the forest.

14 And then my mother use to say to him, "Oh you're always over there for a long time. You always come in at night."

15 She use to be mad.

16 One evening he came home quite late, and we were all sitting around eating.

17 Then he said, "Oh, I seen something strange."

18 "Back in the bush?" my mom says to him. "Yeah," he says. "What did you see over there?" she said to him.

19 And then he told us he seen some children.

20 Little girls running around, not close. He saw them from where he was, way over there.

21 "Running around. Oh, they were really playing," he says to her.

22 "And so I stopped working," he says.

23 "I just stood there and watched them. Ooh they were dressed really nice. And the boys were well dressed." He says.

24 "They looked really good," ya know, "different in the way they dressed."

25   *And um,* "miin'aa ge, zenbaanyin.

26   Wenda go maa mskwaani … *in their* … zenbaanyin gaa-
biiskowaawaanjin maampii.

27   Wenda go gii-minwaanzowag.

28   Wenda gii-boozi-mskwaande iw maa zenbaanyin. Mskoziwan maa
gaa-yaawaawaanjin maa dibaang," dinaan.

29   "Oh, mii-sh go naa maa naaniibwiyaanh gechwaa gegnaa oh," ndig.

30   "Ngii-waabndaan gegoo go naa, gechwaa go naa ni'ii, wiigwaamens
go naa. Gechwaa go naa ngii-waabndaan oodi teg iw," kida.

31   *And ah* … "Mii-sh go iw, mii-sh go naa miin'aa gwekaabwiyaanh mii
gegnaa gii-ngonaagziwaad," kida.

32   "Mii go naa gaa miin'aa ngii-waabmaasiig."

33   "'Aapiish ge iidig gaa-zhaawaad giw,' ndinendam," kido. "Mii go gaa
gonige ngii-waabmaasiig," kida.

34   Mii-sh go naa gii-giizhiitaad enokiid miin'aa gii-bi-maajaad.

35   *And* gii-bi-giiwed mii-sh naa enaajmod megwaa wiisiniyaang.

36   *And ah,* mii-sh go genii gaa-naad iw, "Aaniish ge oodi ge binoojiinyag
bbaanjiptoowaad oodi gtaamgo-waasa go naa?" iw ndinaa. "*Public·
Bush* go naa oodi nikeyaa."

37   "Oh esnaa iidig. Gaawii go gnabaj gegoo binoojiinyag," kida sko naa.

38   *And* gaa go naa gewii go naa gii-debwe'endziin iw binoojiinyag oodi
bbaambatoowaad. Dbi ge-bi-njibaawaagwenh.

25 And um, "also the ribbons.

26 The girls had really bright red ribbons here [pointing to the hair].

27 They were all colored beautifully.

28 The ribbons were colorfully red. They had red in their hair," he says to her.

29 "And while I was standing there," he says to me.

30 "I saw something at a distance. It looked like a little house. I saw something over there," he says.

31 And ah … "Then that's when I turned around and they disappeared," he says.

32 "I didn't see them anymore."

33 "'I wonder where they went,' I thought," he says. "I didn't even see them," he says.

34 Then he just finished what he was doing and he left.

35 And when he came home, that's what he said while we ate.

36 And ah, then she told him, "Why are those kids way out there running around?" I say to him. "Toward Public Bush."

37 "Oh, I don't know. Maybe they weren't children," he says.

38 And he didn't believe they were children running around over there, and he didn't know where they may have come from.

39   Mii-sh go naa e-kidad iw.

40   "Gnabaj go naa, gnabaj go naa," kida, "sko naa giw. 'pa'iinsag,' giw."
      gii-kida. Mii gaa-zhinkaanaad iw.

41   And "Oh, Wenesh ge gewii go naa iw?" ndinaa. "Besha yaawaad giw?"
      ndinaa.

42   Zhaazhi shko naa, kidawag nii iidig go naa giw Nishnaabeg, go naa,
      gaa-bi-yaajig zhaazhi go nwanj nikeyaa."

43   Mii go naa giiwenh giw, mii go naa maa geyaabi bebaa-yaajig.

44   Giw Nishnaabeg miinwaa ni'ii niijaansiwaan.

45   And ah, manj naa iidig, you know, e-nji-zhiyaawaagwenh iw and mii-sh
      go naa genii gaa shki aapji ngii-debwe'endziin ge gwa.

46   Gesnaa mii-sh go ge nmaamaa iw gaa-naad iw, "mii nii naa ezhaayin
      oodi gtaamgo gbe'iing oodi bbaa-yaayin nookming," ndinaan.

47   "Enh, bbaanjiiyaawni oodi niibaadbik," dinaan. "Wiiba gdaa-bi-
      giiwe," dinaan.

48   Oh, gegoo kidsii aw noos. Mii go eta gii-gchi-baapid.

49   "Mii go zhi waa-zhi-yaayin gegoo gwii-oo-waabndaan," dinaan.

50   Mii-sh go iw gaa-naajmod.

39   That's what he said.

40   "Maybe," he says. "those 'little people,'" he said. That's what he called it.

41   And, "Oh, what's that?" I say to him. "Are they close to here?" I say to him.

42   Long time ago, Nishnaabeg said they were here, further in the past.

43   Apparently, they're still around.

44   Those Nishnaabeg and their children.

45   And ah, I'm not sure, you know, why they feel that way, and I didn't really believe it.

46   So then my mom told him, "That's because you go over there for too long, around in the bush," she tells him.

47   "Yeah, I don't know why you're out there at night," she says to him. "You should come home early," she tells him.

48   Oh, my dad didn't say anything. He just laughed.

49   "That's what going to happen to you. You're going to see something," she says to him.

50   That's what he talked about.

MII SA GO IIDIG 'GONDA'

1   Miin'aa gshko gewii ngoding na'aa nzigos ge ngoding gii-ke-bbaa ...,
    gii-dzhimaad go niw.

2   Enh, oodi nikeyaa. Ni'ii ziibiing nikeyaa gii-daawag.

3   Aazhwaakwaa. Maa dash dibziibi nikeyaa gii-daawag.

4   Pane shko naa ngii-zhaami.

5   Ngoding shko naa zhaayaang oodi pane go naa oodi nikeyaa Nelson
    Zhognosh endaad, miin'aa Dan Zhognosh gii-daawaad.

6   Mii-sh naa nookmimensing maa naa ni'ii mii go naa maampii
    wiigwaam temgak.

7   Mii-sh maa zhizhyaaw maa gii-bminabtoowag.

8   Gaawii go naa oodi miikanaang.

9   Zhizhyaaw maa gii-bmi-zhaawag.

10 Mii-sh go oodi bmizaakmowaad oodi ya'aa Nelson Zhognosh gnabaj
    ngoji gaa-ndaad.

11 Mii-sh go naa ko oodi gaa-zhaad ii pane go gii-aabjitoonaawaa
    miikaans.

12 Zhaazhi ge go naa mii gaa-zhichgewaad iw, *ya know*, ninwag ko gii-
    bminabtoowag zhizhyaaw wii-bbaa-zhaawaad ngojii.

IT'S PROBABLY "THEM"

1 And also, once um, my aunty talked about them once, too.

2 Over there. They lived toward the river.

3 Backsettlement. So they lived near the edge of the river.

4 We always went there.

5 At one time, we always went over that way, Nelson Zhognosh's house, and Dan Zhognosh, they lived there.

6 In that little bush there, that's here where the house is.

7 Then they'd run straight through.

8 Not on the road.

9 They'd go straight through there.

10 Then they came out [appeared] over somewhere near where Nelson Zhognosh lived.

11 Then after he went over there, we would always use the trail.

12 Long time ago they did that, ya know. They walked straight through to wherever they were going.

13   Nookming. Dbi go naa iidig. Gaa go memkaach miiknaang.

14   Mii dash gaa-zhi-yaayaang ngoding iw "oh" mii dash ekidod iw, "Oh,
      ka-zhaami wodi, ya'aa, Dan Zhognosh endaad. Aabdeg gwii-zhaami."

15   Oh mii sa naa gii-bmi-zhiitaawaad. Oh mii-sh go naa maa
      enakmigziyaang go naa, mii-sh go naa gewii gegaa wii-ni-naakshig.

16   "Oh wewiib gsha go naa ndaa-ni-maajaami," kidawag.

17   Mii-sh go wewiib ge ni-maajaayaang.

18   Mii-sh go maa gaa-ni-zhaayaang maa, kina go naa ngii-maawnidmi
      zhaayaang oodi.

19   Ko gegnaa znagsinoo maa gaa-ni-namoog. Mii go naa zhizhyaaw go
      naa gegaa.

20   *Ya know.* Gaawii go naa nikeyaa maanda gii-naaksinoo waa-ni-zhaayaang.

21   Yooo mii gsha go naa ngii-gchi-bmosemi gbe'iing go naa.

22   Ooo mii naa ko maa zhaayaang oodi mii go miinwaa oodi, nda-*auntie*
      da mii go naa gaa-ni-niigaaniid.

23   Mii-sh go iw ekidod iw "Aaniish go naa!" Kida, "Aapiish go naa
      maanda ni-zaag'mok maanda ni'ii miikaans?" kida gaa go naa ngojii
      nmakziinaa iw, *you know.*

24   Mii-sh go naa iw, manj naa iidig naa, gaa-zhiyaawngide mii go naa eta
      maa gii-bmoseyaang maampii-sh go naa.

25   "Mii sa go iidig 'gonda'!" kida.

26   "Mii go iidig maaba. Yaawag nii naa go maampii giw," kida. "Pa'iinsag."

13   In the bush. Anywhere [in the bush]. Not necessarily on the road.

14   And then, one time when we were over there, "Oh," he then said that. "Oh, let's go over there, um, to Dan Zhognosh's house. We have to go there."

15   They started getting ready. So we got busy with things, and it started to be the evening.

16   "Oh, hurry up, we should leave," they said.

17   So we left in a hurry.

18   Then we started going over there; we went together over there.

19   It wasn't difficult to be led through the path. It was almost straight.

20   Ya know. It didn't look this way, the way we went through.

21   Yooo we walked for a long time.

22   Ooo, that's the way we use to go there many times, and my auntie was leading.

23   And then she said, "What the heck!" She says, "Where the heck does this path end?" she says. We couldn't find it.

24   Then that, I don't know what happened to us. All we did was walk along here.

25   "It's probably 'them'!" she says.

26   "It's probably this one. They're probably here," she says. "Little people."

27   Mii dash, "mii go maaba maa emgoshkaajtaad maa kida "Gdaa-
      wnishmigonaa go naa," kidawag nii.

28   Mii dash gii-giishkshwaad ni' semaan. Gii-...*pluck*. Ni'ii go naa *square*
      one go naa ow.

29   Iw shaashaagmind dnowa. Mii niw dnowa pane go bmi-yaawaanjin.

30   Mii dash ndawaach gii-...mshkimdaang gii-ndowaabmaad niw.

31   Oh gii-giishkshwaad pane gegoo gii-bmi-yaan mookmaanens.

32   Mii-sh oodi dowa gii-ow-saad niw.

33   "Maaba! Nendowendang!" gii-naan niw. "Oh booniikwishinaang
      dash!" gii-naan. "Zhaazhi gii-miinin nendwendman."

34   Mii niinwi ko go maa gaa-bmi-dzhi-gyakseyaang maa miin'aa gii-
      bmizaakiiyaang oodi iw miiknaang, *ya know*?

35   Gaa go naa memdige go naa waasa ngii-yaasiimi.

36   *And*...mii-sh go naa genii *ya know. I thought* "Aaniish ge iidig mii
      naa mekwendmaanh iw?" *Ya know*, "noos oodi gii-waabmaapa niw
      gwegwendig go naa giw mii go naa iidig pa'iinsag."

37   *And I said*, "Oh geget sa naa!" ndinaa. "Mii go naa iidig geget ezhi-aawi
      ...ezhi-aawiwaad giw," ndikid.

38   Mii go naa iidig yaawaad maa nookmensing. Mii-sh go naa pii
      dbaajmowaad niw. Ninwag gegoo gii-dbaajmaawaan ko niw.
      Waabmaawaad.

39   Mii-sh go naa genii gaa-nendmaanh iw.

40   "Mii sko naa iidig giw" ndinendam.

27   Then, "That's the one that's disruptive," she says. "They can even get us lost," they said.

28   Then she cut up some tobacco. She plucked it. A square one [tobacco].

29   The chewing kind. That's the kind they always had.

30   Then she looked for it in her bag instead.

31   Oh, she was always cutting with that little knife.

32   Then she put that down over there.

33   "This! This is what he wants!" she told them [the pa'iinsag]. "Oh leave us alone now!" she told them. "I already gave you what you want."

34   And then we walked the right way and we came out on the road there.

35   We weren't that far [from the road].

36   Then I too, thought "Why didn't I think of that too?" Ya know, "My dad had seen them, whoever, must have been those pa'iinsag."

37   And I said, "Oh for goodness sakes!" I say to her. "That's must really … really be them," I said.

38   They must have been there in the little bush. That's when they talk about those things. The men use to talk about them. Who they saw.

39   That's what I remembered.

40   "So that must be them," I thought.

41   Endgwenh sha noongwa wii-yaawaagwenh gaa go naa wiya
      dbaajmosii noongwa wii-waabmaad ge niw.

42   Gaa-sh ge go naa wii-nookming noongwa bbaa-yaasii.

43   Zhaazhi wii go naa pane ninwag nookming gii-nakmigziwaad.
      Giishkboojgewaad, daawewaad mitigoon, mii go naa pane oodi
      gii-baa-yaawaad.

41   So I don't know if they're around now. No talks about seeing them.

42   Well no one's around in the bush these days.

43   Long time ago the men worked in the bush. They logged, sold the wood, they were always around over there.

MII OW ZHAAGNAASHAG MAAMPII WAA-BI-YAAJIG

1 Enh, mii sa genii iw eni-dzhindmaanh.

2 Mii na ge go naa ko maanda ayaa nookmis miinwaa mishoomis
   ko gii-noondwaa go naa naan'gidoonwaad giw maanda waa-ni-
   zhiwebak niigaan kina nikeyaa.

3 Gii-waabndaanaawaa.

4 Gaa wiikaa ngii-debwetwaasii. "Aaniish ge-zhi-gkendmowaad waa-
   ni-zhiwebak gegoo," ndinendam

5 Maanda nbiish noongwa. Gaa maamdaa wii-mnikweying. Aabdeg
   gwii-giishnadoonaa.

6 Mii go gaa-kidad iw.

7 Enh, ngoding sa niinwi. "Mii waa-zhiwebak," gii-kida. "Gwii-
   giishnadoonaa nbiish waa-mnikweying."

8 "Aaniish ge iidig waa-zhi-giishnadooying?" ndikid.

9 "Baatiinad swii maampii nbiish mena go naa dig" ndinendam.

10 You know, ngii-maamkaaztowaa go naa gii-kidad i'.

11 "Ah gesganaa maa gegnaa nishaa go naa ekidowaagwenh," ngii-
   nendam.

THE WHITE PEOPLE WILL BE HERE

1   Yeah, that's what I started to talk about.

2   This is what I use to hear from grandmother and grandfather when
    they talked about what was going to happen in the future.

3   They saw it.

4   I never believed it. "How do they know what was going to happen?"
    I thought.

5   This water now. We aren't able to drink it. We have to buy it.

6   That's what they said.

7   Yeah, one day for us, "That's what's going to happen," they said.
    "We're going to buy water to drink."

8   "How is it possible that we're going to have to buy water?" I said.

9   "But there lots of water all over here," I thought.

10 You know, I was surprised to hear that he said that.

11 "Oh they must be just joking saying that," I thought.

12 Nooj go naa ko gegoo gii-kida iw nikeyaa waa-ni-zhiwebak niigaan nikeyaa.

13 Miin'aa geǵnaa mii go gaa-kidad ge "oh zhaagnaashag wii-ni-baatiinwag maampii" gii-kidawag ge.

14 *You know*, "gaawii eta nishnaabeg. Mii ow zhaagnaashag maampii waa-ni-yaajig," gii-kida.

15 Mii-sh go noongwa ezhi-kendmaanh iw.

16 *You know*, kina go naa noongwa zhaagnaashag maampii enkiijig.

17 Miin'aa go naa endaajig da-ni-zhitoonaawaan wiigwaaman and miin'aa shko ngoding gii-kida "Oh miin'aa giw ni'ii jiimaan go naa gegaa go gwegwendig go naa zhinkaadmagwenh iw wii-bmibde shpiming," kida.

18 "Oh, Mii go da-wii-bmi-wiisiniwaad bemaadzijig," kida.

19 *You know*, "waasa ezhaajig. Mii oodi wii-bmi-wiisiniwaad," kida. "Onh, mii waa-ni-zhiwebak," iw-gii-kida.

20 Gaa-sh go naa genii gaa ndebwetawaasii, *you know*, gekaanyag go naa, mii naan'godnong mii enendmang iw. "Gaa go naa gkendziinaawaa naan'gidoonwaad go naa" ndinendam ko geniin.

21 (Jennie Blackbird) 'Mbaashjigan.'

22 Enh, gwegwendig go naa iw gaa-zhinkaadang iw '*airplane*' go naa.

23 Mii dash iw gaa-kidad iw, "Oh wii-mbaawag miin'aa wii-wiisiniwag oodi megwaa bmibziwaad," gii-kida.

24 Mii-sh go noongo ezhiwebak iw.

12 They use to say various things that were going to happen in the future.

13 And they would say, "Oh there going to be lots of white people here," they'd say that too.

14 You know, "Not just Anishinaabe people. The white people will be here," they said.

15 And now that's what I know today.

16 You know, all the white people are workers here.

17 And the ones living here build the houses, and one time they said, "Oh, and it's like a ship, I don't know what they're called, the things will be flying up high," he said.

18 "Oh, they'll be traveling along eating," he says.

19 You know, "They go far. They're going to be going along eating over there," he says. "Oh, that's what's going to happen," he says.

20 I didn't really believe them, you know, the elders, sometimes that's what we think. "They don't know what they were talking about," I use to think.

21 (Jennie Blackbird) "Mbaashjigan."

22 Yeah, I'm not not sure what one calls an "airplane."

23 That's what they said, "Oh they're going go to sleep and they're going to eat while they're flying," they said.

24 Now that's happening today.

25   Mii-sh go naa genii eta memdige go naa iw waa-ni-kidayaanh maa genii emnjimendamaanh kina gegoo gaa-bi-zhi-noondamaanh gegoo miin'aa gaa-bi-zhi-gkenmagwaa nooj iidig ezhi-yaajig nookming.

26   Ngii-wnishinami go naa maa besha ge go naa maa ni-zhaayaang.

27   Ngii-maamkaadendam go genii gii-zhi-yaayaang "aaniish ge!" ndinendam.

28   Mii-sh iw eta genii waa-naajmoyaanh iw. *And*, mii go naa … mii go naa iw minik.

25   That's about all I want to say about what I remember about
      everything that I heard and how I knew about those ones that are in
      the bush.

26   We got lost when were on our way close to there.

27   I was surprised too, when we ended up there. "What else [could
      happen]!" I thought.

28   That's all I want to talk about. And, that's about it.

Doopinibiikwe

Linda George gii-dbaajma / Stories told by Linda George

GAA-BAAMSEWAAD DIBIKAK GIW KWEWAG

1 Doopinibiikwe ndizhinikaaz, Linda George nishaagnaashiiwnikaazayaanh.

2 Maanda dash waa-dbaajdamaanh maaba bezhig shkiniikwe ngii-bi-mbwaach'ig. Mii dash iw gii-kwejimid iw gegoo go naa wii-dzhindmaanh iw, wii-dbaajdamaanh.

3 Mii dash iw ngii-dbaajdaan shkwaa ... giishenh gegoo ngii-dbaajim miin'aa gii-ni-dbaajdamaanh iw.

4 Wenda shko ngii-maamiiktaag.

5 Mii dash gaa-zhid iw, gdaa ... niin go naa ... giishpin iw wii-wiindmaageyin ... ni'ii go naa gdaa-mzinaa ... aanii ge naa? ...

6 "Gdaa-mzinaakshkow 'di" ... manj go naa iidig-sh ... "they can record," ngii-ig sko naa. "Giishpin wii-wiindmaageyin iw," ngii-ig. "onh" ndinaa. "Ahaaw," ngii-naa.

7 Mii dash gii-dbaajmoyaanh iw,' gonda na'aag Medewaadzijig.

8 Mii ko gaa-kidad ow na'aa noosba iw gii-dzhimaad miin'aa go, zhaazhi sko naa giw noosba, mishoomis, nookmis, kina go gii-dbaajdaanaawaa maanda.

9 Oodi ko ni'iing Aazhwaakwaa oodi ni'iing miikan oodi bezhig gii-ninimod widi ni'iing Aazhwaakwaa nikeyaa.

WHEN THOSE WOMEN WALKED AROUND AT NIGHT

1 Doopinibiikwe is my name. Linda George is what I'm called in English.

2 So what I'm going to talk about … is how this one young woman came to visit me and asked me to talk about something.

3 Well I talked a little bit about everything.

4 She was really interested in what I talked about.

5 Then she said to me … me … if you want to tell that story … you could … how is that said? …

6 "You can make a printing of me [what I say] over there," … I'm not sure [how to say it] … "They can record," she told me. "If you want to talk about that," she told me. "Oh," I say to her. "OK," I told her.

7 Then I talked about these Midewiwin/traditional people.

8 That's what my dad use to say when he talked about them. Long time ago my dad, my grandfather, my grandmother talked about this.

9 They talked about this one road that goes toward backsettlement back there.

10   Mii dash giiwenh maa gii-yaamigad ni'ii jiibegamik ki.

11   Mii dash iw ... mii dash giiwenh maa giw kina, mii-sh go eta gaa-
      naabjitoowaad kina maa giw Medewaadzijig gii-bgidendiwag.

12   Mii go naa gonda ge-bwaa-debwe'endagig nam'aawin ge go naa
      ganamaa nikeyaa. 'Pagens' go naa gii-zhinkaanaawaan niwi.

13   Mii-sh go wiya nbod mii nbowaad go naa gewiinwaa gaa-
      zhitwaawaad mii oodi, mii go eta gaa-sijgaazajig.

14   Mii dash ngoding iw giiwenh na'aa go naa oodi gii-daawag oh
      aapji-sh shkwe'iing oodi na'aa, Blackbirds gii-zhinkaazawag na'aa
      Elijah Blackbird.

15   Kina go dzhiindwind biweziiman niw idi kina gii-daawaad. Isabelle
      gii-zhinkaazwan na'aa, wiiwan miinwaa giw Mkade-bineshiiyag
      gii-zhinkaazook gii-shkiniikwewaad giwi.

16   Mii dash giiwenh ngoding iw waasa shko naa waa-zhi-bmosewaad.
      Mii-sh ko iw gii-niibaaptoowaad ko wedi gewiinwaa mii iw mii sko
      gii-bi ... gaa-bi-ndosewaad oodi.

17   Mii dash giiwenh iw, mii-sh ko ganamaa maampii gegnaa ganamaa
      gaa-zhaawaagwenh mii gegnaa maampii maage go naa wodi.

18   Mii-sh giiwenh ko gaa-naad ow Isabelle. "Naasanaa, naasanaa wiiba
      naa ga-bi-yaa jibwaa ni-dibikak," gii-naan giiwenh ko. Ah, mii shko
      gii naa gaa-bzindziiwag "oh ahaaw. Ahaaw." Mii go eta gaa-kidwaad
      maajaawaad.

19   Oh mii-shii go naa da gaa-bmi-dzhi-dbikdinik, mii-sh naa pii waa-bi-
      giiwewaad.

20   Ah mii sa giiwenh naabwaad idi miiknaang. "Oh geget sa naa oodi
      waasa bmoseying" gii-kidwag giiwenh.

10   There was a cemetery there.

11   And then that...and then apparently only the Midewiwin people were the ones who used it, when they had buried ones who passed.

12   These are the ones that didn't believe in Christianity. They called them "pagans."

13   When anyone of them died that were Midewiwin, they'd made that for them, they were the only ones that were put there.

14   And then one time they said there were people living at the end of the road, they were the Blackbird family. Elijah Blackbird.

15   The whole family lived over there. Isabelle was his wife's name. And girls that were young were called Blackbird girls.

16   So one time they had to walk home a quite a ways, when they were running around all night. And then...they had to walk back from there.

17   I don't know where they would go, over here or over there.

18   Isabelle use to tell them, "Be careful, get home before dark." She use to tell them that, but they didn't listen. "OK, OK." that's all they said when they left.

19   Then when it got dark, that is when it was time for them to come back home.

20   They looked down the road. "Oh gosh, it's a long ways we have to walk," they said.

21   Gii-gkendaanaawaa maa jiibegamik ki yaanig. Mii dash gotaanaawaa
     maa wii-ni-bmosewaad.

22   Yaamigad-sh giiwenh go maa gii-ntaagod iw ni'ii jiibegmiki.

23   Mii dash aabdeg waa-ni-zhaawaad gaa go maamdaa ngoji waa-ni-
     zhaawaad.

24   Oh mii sa giiwenh ko gii-gtamwaad. Oh mii-sh go naa go wedi
     maanoo gii-ni-maajaawaad. Oh mii-sh go naa ko wewiib gii-
     bmosewaad.

25   Naangodnong gii-bmiptoowag gewe wii … wii-ni-dgoshnowaad
     maa naa ni'ii. Gii-noondaanaawaa go nii naa giiwenh ko gegoo maa.
     Gii-ntaagod go naa iw ni'ii jiibegamik ki.

26   Mii dash giiwenh … mii-sh go gaa-kidwaad mii giiwenh ko gii-…,
     wiya go naa nbod oodi ow ezhtoowaad gii-… mii go naa gaa-shkwaa-
     ngogaazad maapiich go naa mii giiwenh ko gaa-zhi-gtaakmiseg ni
     ni'iin jiibegamigoon.

27   *They use to cave in,* 'gtaakmiseg.' Mii-sh giiwenh ko ya'aa go maa
     maapiich go naa ya'aa-sh giiwenh ko maa gii-zaagdoodewag
     gnebigoog.

28   Gii-zaagdoodewaad maa jiibegamik, maa go naa, ganamaa gaa-
     bgidenmind. "Oh aaniish ge iidig," gii-kidook-sh giiwenh ko gaa-
     ndzhi-yaamgak aanind ni'ii jiibegmigoon.

29   "Manj sa naa iidig," kidook mii-sh wii go naa iidig ni'ii gaa-
     piichi-mshkawziimigadnig ni'ii mshkiki gaa-gkendmowaad giw,
     Midewaadziwag maa naa.

30   Mii ko gaa-kidwaad gii-gaa-kidad iw gaa-zhi-noondmaanh genii.

21   They know that that cemetery is there. They were afraid to walk by it.

22   They said that graveyard was haunted.

23   Well they have to walk down that road, there's no other way to go [to get home].

24   Oh, well they were afraid, but that's where they have to go, so they started walking. Then they use to walk in a hurry.

25   Sometimes they ran ... to arrive there [quicker]. They use to hear things there. That cemetery was haunted.

26   And apparently ... they use to say, apparently ... that when someone died, ... the Midewiwin people buried them there. And eventually (when the grave got older) it use to cave in.

27   They use to cave in, "gtaakmiseg." After a while, there were snakes crawling out of the grave.

28   Whoever was buried there, the snakes came out of that grave. "What the heck?" they supposedly said when they use to wonder why that happened to the graves.

29   "I don't know," they said, but after a while they thought it must have been that strong medicine that the Midewiwin people knew, maybe.

30   That's what I use to hear them say.

31   Mii ge go naa iw … mii giiwenh go naa iw ni'ii gaa-nji-
      zaagdoodewaad maa ge gnebigoog. Mii go naa i' mshkiki … mji-
      mshkiki gaa-gkendmowaad gewe.

32   Mii ko gaa-kidwaad iw.

33   Ngoding-sh giiwenh, ngoding-sh giiwenh maa wiya go naa gii-nboba
      mii-sh giiwenh oodi miin'aa maa gegnaa mii go naa enwemaawaajin
      giw Medewaadzijig.

34   Mii-sh go ge di gaa-zhiwnindoon gii-bgidenmind. Mii-sh giiwenh
      giw bgidenmind oodi.

35   Mii-sh giiwenh maapiich go naa mii giiwenh mii giiwenh ko pane
      gaa-zhi-gonaajwang iw ni'ii jiibegamik.

36   Gaa wiikaa gii-naazhsesinoo wii-gtaakmiseg. Mii go pane gaa-zhi-
      gonaajwang gii-shpaawngising.

37   Mii go pane gaa-zhi-gonaajwang giiwenh, ni'ii, jiibegamik.

38   Mii-sh giiwenh miin'aa ekdawaad "Onh, aaniish ge gaawii iw gegoo
      zhiyaasinoo jiibegamik," gii-kido giiwenh.

39   "Aaniish ge iidig?" Aaniish giiwenh maaba bezhig gii-kida "Oh,
      gii-nam'aa sa niin naa maa gaa-oo-bgidenmind," gii-kida-sh giiwenh
      maaba bezhig.

40   "Aapji go gii-nam'aa maaba. Kwe maage nini, gaa go naa ngii-
      gkendziin."

41   Mii dash iw gaawii, gaa go gnebig maa ge waabnjigaazsii.

42   Mii dash. Mii-sh giiwenh gaa-nji-gyakwang iw ni'ii jiibegamik. Mii
      go pane gaa-zhinaagok iw.

31   That's also … that's supposedly why the snakes crawled out of there.
      It's that medicine … that bad medicine that they knew.

32   That's what they use to say.

33   One time someone died and maybe the Midewiwin people were
      related to this person [he wasn't Midewiwin].

34   They took him over there to bury him. So apparently, he got buried
      there.

35   So supposedly, eventually that grave was always the same; it was
      nice.

36   It never sank down or caved in. It was always nice; it was always a
      mound.

37   It was always nice, that grave.

38   So they said, "Oh, there's nothing wrong with that graveyard." They
      said, apparently.

39   "Why?" This one person supposedly said, "Oh this man was a
      Christian that was buried here," he said, supposedly.

40   "This person was a real good Christian. I don't know if he or she was a
      man or woman."

41   So, a snake wasn't seen [near that grave].

42   That's apparently why that one grave looked good. That's how it
      looked all the time.

43 Mii-sh ii go naa aanind gtaakmiseg mii dash maa giw mnidooshag
gii-zaagdoodewaad.

44 Mii i' ngoding iw gaa-…mii ko gaa-kidwaad maa.

45 Mii dash iidig gaa-ni-nji-zegziwaad ko maa bmosewaad giw
na'aa mkade-bineshiikweyag naazh go ko ngii-wiindmaagnaa iw.
Na'aa bmosewaad maa naa ko 'Una' gii-zhinikaaza maa ow. Gii-
shkiniikwewshowaad.

46 Mii iw…mii gaa…gii-noondaanaawaa giiwenh ko gegoo maa
ngoding gegoo maa ge gechwaa naa wiya bi-yaawan shkweyaang
bmosewaad maa.

47 Oh mii-sh go iidig, gaa-sh ge gwa aabnaabisiiwag.

48 Oh mii-sh giiwenh go naa, oh wewiib gwetaansewag.

49 Enh, maampii go naa ge gii-ni-bmiptóowaad.

50 Mii-sh go naa maampii go naa yekziwaad iidig bmiptoo miinwaa
gii-nookshkaawaad.

51 Mii-sh giiwenh gii…kawe gaa-naaniibwiwaad maa kina gegoo
wii-noondwaawaad biidweweshininid.

52 Gaa-sh giiwenh gwa naa wiya.

53 Mii-sh giiwenh pii oodi dbi naa iidig gaa-ni-dgoshnawaad mii-sh
kina dbaajmowaad idi mii ni-zegziwaad.

54 Gii-nchiiwchigaazawag-sh giiwenh. Ow Isabelle gii-nchiiwaad.

55 "Oh aaniinde oodi, gyak sa go…," odinaan giiyenh. "Gyak sa go
gii-bi-zegziyeg oodi. Gii-bi-zegigwaag ow na'aag oodi engogaazajig,"
gii-naan giiwenh.

43   And then the other ones would cave in and bugs would crawl out of them.

44   That's what was once ... that's what they use to say about that there.

45   Why those Blackbird girls were scared to walk through there since we were told that [it was haunted] when they walked. Una was her name. When they were young girls,

46   That's what ... that's ... they use to hear strange noises there, and one time they thought someone was coming behind them.

47   They didn't want to turn around and look.

48   Oh and they really walked fast.

49   Later on they just started running.

50   Later on they were running and got tired so they had to stop and rest.

51   So supposedly ... then when they were standing there they were listening for someone that made a noise coming toward them.

52   [They checked to see if someone was coming.] But no one was there.

53   After they arrived home they must have told them their experience of getting scared.

54   They got a scolding, apparently. Then Isabelle scolded them.

55   "Oh, of course that's good [you walked by] over there ...," she said to them. "That's good, that you got scared, that the ones buried over there scared you," she apparently told them.

56   "Pane sa aana gdinnim wodi wii-bwaa-bi-bmoseyeg 'naasanaa wii-bi-dgoshnok' gdinnim gaa gdaa-bzindziim."

57   Mii dash iw gaa-…Mii naa ko gaa…Mii ko gewii go iw Una gaa-kidpa dbaajdizwaad go naa gii-shkiniikwewshowaad.

58   Mii ko iidig…mii-sh giiwenh go ngoji miin'aa gii-zhaa miin'aa maajaawaad niibaadbik. Kizheb sko naa manj maa naa maampii maajaa nenaakshinig.

59   Oh mii go wewiib gii-bi-bskaabiiwaad jibwaa aapji-ni-dbikak. Mii go naa wii-bwaa-ni-zegziwaad maa.

60   Aanind shko mii go gaa-damwaad ni'iin maampii ge go bezhig Aazhwaakwaa maa na'iing *campground* gii-zhinkaade iw.

61   Ge wii go ko maa gii-zegziwag gaa-bmosejig.

62   Na'aa giiwenh…{*isn't there a little graveyard there?*}…enh, gnabaj gwa.

63   Dnawa go niinaa gii-yaanoon ni'ii jiibegamikiin. Zhaazhi go naa gii-bgidendiwaad.

64   Noongwa niinaa gaawiin mii go naa eta oodi highbank.

56 "I always told you all to not walk by there [after dark] and to be careful arriving here, but you guys wouldn't listen."

57 So that's what … That's what use to … That's what Una use to say when they told stories about themselves when they were young.

58 That's what might've … So that's apparently when they went to go somewhere whether it was in the morning or during the evening.

59 They went right home before dark so they wouldn't be scared walking through there again.

60 Some people talked about here in backsettlement, the campground, it's called.

61 They ones who walked by there use to get scared too.

62 Apparently, {isn't there a little graveyard there?}. Yeah, probably.

63 There were graveyards all over, where they buried them there long time ago.

64 Nowadays they don't, only at Highbanks [place on Bkejwanong].

GII-NI-ZEGZI-SH GO GEWII WIYA
GII-GWIISHKSHIMGOON OODI

1   Nawaj go naa go gii-zhi-yaawag go naa.

2   Ngashi ge go ngoding maampii mii go naa jiigbiig iw yaanoon.

3   Ge go mii go iw naa ni'ii yaamgak maa iw binoojiinyag enji-gnawenmindwaa.

4   Mii go maa iw. Mii go ge ngoding maa bi-bmosed niibaadbik.

5   Oodi maa naa gii-nokiiwag gaaming bemaadzijig. Mii-sh ge wedi bi-njibaad.

6   Mii-sh go gewii oodi maa naa gaa-niimidwaagwenh wodi ni'ii Parish Hall.

7   Mii wodi ko gewii gii-bi-nookshkaad.

8   Waabnjiged go naa. Mii-sh go ge maa miin'aa ni-bmosed maa shpide-dbik.

9   Gii-ni-zegzi shko gewii wiya gii-gwiishkshimgoon oodi.

10 "Oh mii-sh go naa gesnaa gegoo na bi-zhiyaa," kida. Enh.

11 Miin'aa dash maa ni'ii mjikan go naa maa gii-yaa miin'aa maa ni'ii gate. Gchi-ngate.

SHE GOT SCARED TOO WHEN SOMEONE WHISTLED AT HER OVER THERE

1   There were different experiences at different places I guess.

2   One time, my mother was up at the beach,

3   Where the children's daycare is. [Where the children are, there's a graveyard.]

4   It's there. She was walking back during the night one time.

5   Since they worked across the lake [United States], she was coming from there.

6   So over there they might have been dancing at Parish Hall.

7   That's where she use to stop.

8   She just watched. She had to walk from there late at night.

9   She got scared, too, when someone whistled at her over there.

10 "Oh, [I was sensing] something was coming," she said. Yeah.

11 And then was a fence there and um a gate, a big gate.

12   "Mii-sh go naa maanda bmoseyaanh maanda naanind oh gechwaa
     wiya naaniibwi oodi gnawaabmid," kida. "Oodi nikeyaa wa-ndi-
     naabiyaanh gechwaa go naa wiya widi naaniibwi," kida,

13   "Oh, mii sa niin ge bmi-dkonaanan ni'iin gaa … gii-oodetooyaanh,"
     kida. Ni'ii maa eta mzinigini- ni'ii gii-ntaasiwag. "Oh bmi-dkonaan.
     Oh wenda go naa ge niw gchi-mnjimnaanan," kida.

14   "Oh eya piiskaayaanh gaa ge maamdaa bmiptooyaanh bmi-
     dkomaanh niwi," kida.

15   "Oh geget sa naa gegoo gonaa ndizhayaa gechwaa go naa wiya ndaa-
     bi-daangnig oodi ni'ii shkweyaang," kida. "Ooonh aya piitzi-."

16   "Maapii-sh naa miinwaa go naa ngii-noondwaa wiya oodi-sh nikeyaa
     nii-nkweshkwaa wiya," kida. "Mii-sh gii-ni-booni-zegziyaanh."

17   "Gechwaa naa oodi wii-bi-njikse wiya," nendam giiwenh. Bmose-sh
     go.

18   Mii-sh aa iidig mbe naa go naa iidig gii-ni-zhiyaad wiya oodi ngii-
     waabmaad oodi nikeyaa bi-njibaanid.

19   Gii-nkweshkwaad giiwenh maa.

20   Ya'aa oodi shko naa ge nikeyaa gii-bmozwaa neniizh shkonaa
     gwegwendig gegnaa kida wa-bmose maa.

21   "Mii sa wiintam oodi wii-ni-zegizid," gii-kida-sh giiwenh.

22   "Mii wiintam oodi ji-ni-zegigod niwi gwegwendigenan," kida
     giiwenh.

23   Nendam skonaa giiwenh, "oh mii-sh go aana go gii-ni-giiwed iidig."

12   "So when I walked by there, I seen someone standing by the gate looking at me," she said. "Well, I looked over there and it looked like someone was standing over there," she said.

13   "Oh, I was carrying things … [groceries] I got from shopping over there," she said. There were only cardboard and glass. "Oh, I carried that. I was hanging onto them tight," she said.

14   "Oh I walked really fast. I couldn't run because I was carrying those [bags]," she said.

15   "I felt really afraid, I thought someone was going to touch me on my back," she said. "Oh that's how [scared I was]."

16   "Finally, I heard someone in the other direction, I was going to meet them," she said. "I quit being afraid."

17   "Seems like someone was going to appear," she thought. So she was still walking.

18   She felt better because she saw someone coming from the other way.

19   She apparently met this man there.

20   He was walking on the other side, and she thought,

21   "Oh gosh, he's going to be the next one getting scared," she apparently said.

22   "Whoever is over there will scare him too," she supposedly said.

23   She thought, "Oh I can probably make it home."

24 Naa go ngoding oodi ni'iing Fred Emptinja store maa gii-yaan maa *corner*.

25 Mii ge ngoding maa gii-ni-dbendawaad niwi, kiwenziinyin.

26 Mii go gii-ni-zegizid. Gaawii wii-ni-giiwesii.

27 Gii-detewaakoged oodi.

28 Daa-yaa naa go naa maampii.

29 "Gegoo idi ngii-noondaan," kida giiwenh. "Gii-yaa go naa wiya gonaa da gechwaa go naa biidwewebtood," kida. "miinwaa ningbiginwenh gchi-noondaagzid," kida.

30 Oh mii-sh go naa gii-zegizid iidig. Mii go oodi nikeyaa waa-ni-zhaad.

31 Mii-sh go naa oodi gewii wewiib oodi gii-patood detewaakoge kiwenziinh. "Oh gaa gewii wewiib oodi bi-nsaaknaziinan," ow kida.

32 "Aa wiikaa sa naasanaa oodi biidweweshing kidni bi-gaaskzideboozad," kida.

33 Ah bi-nsaaknaan esnaa gaawaanh gwa. "Oh, bi-nsaaknaan," kida. "'Onh, wene dash iidig gewii ow?' kida."

34 "Oh, wewiib nii-biindge. Wiya gsha go naa gechwaa go naa oodi biidwewebtoo," wdinaan giiwenh.

35 "Oh," kida giiwenh. "Ahaaw." Mii-sh gii–nsaaknang. Ndinaa.

36 Mii-sh go naa da maa ni'ii go naa maa gwiidibiwin ni'ii sko naa iw go naa iw, *couch* go naa gechwaa.

37 "Mii maa gii-nmadbiseyaanh," kida. "gii-nmadabiyaanh maa," kida. "oh wenda go naa nzegiz," kida.

24   Once she got to the four corners Fred Ermatinger's store.

25   So once she stayed over night there, the old man's place.

26   She was starting to get scared. She didn't want to go home.

27   She went knocking on that old man's door.

28   He should be here.

29   "I heard something over there," she said. "Like someone was running this way," she said. "And a screech owl making a lot of noise."

30   Oh, she really got scared because that's the direction she wanted to go.

31   When she quickly ran to that old man's house, she knocked. "Oh, he wouldn't answer right away," she said.

32   "I finally heard him coming. His feet shuffling to the door," she said.

33   He barely opened the door. "Oh, he opened the door," she said. "'Oh, who is it?' he said."

34   "Oh, I want to come in quickly. I hear someone running this way," she told him, apparently.

35   "Oh," he said. "OK." Then he opened the door.

36   There was a chair there, like a couch.

37   "That's where I sat [flopped down on]," she said. "I sat there," she said. "Oh I was really scared."

38 Mii-sh go maa, "'oh gdaa-ni-aadaakwan iw ni-maajaayin,' ndig-sh 'miin'aa ow shkwaandem,'" kida. "Oh mii-sh wii go naa mii go naa maa aadshinaanh." kida.

39 "Wenda go ngii-zegiz," kida. "Mii go baa maa gaa-waabang, weweni go gaa-waabang. Mii gii-bi-maajaayaanh," kida.

40 "Gchi-baapi sa ow kiwenziinh," dinaa.

41 Mii sa iw minik genii ow waa-naajmoyaanh iw.

38   Then, "'Oh, you can lock that when you leave,' he said to me. 'That door,'" she said." Oh, this is where I'm stuck," she said.

39   "I was really scared," she said. "I didn't leave until morning. Early the next morning, that's when I left," she said.

40   "That old man just laughed," she said.

41   Well that's about all I want to talk about.

Noodin

Eric Isaac gii-dbaajma / Stories told by Eric Isaac

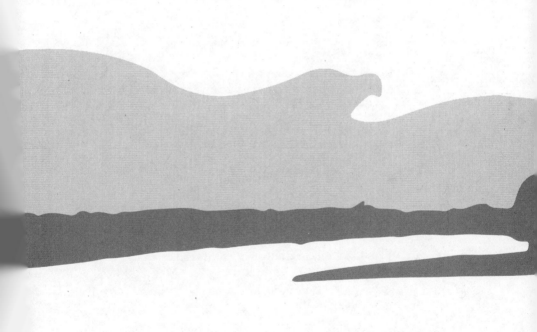

JIIWEGAANH DBAAJMOWIN

1   Ahaaw, maajtaami, nii nishnaabemyaang maampii. Noodin niin, ndizhinikaaz.

2   Anishnaabewinikaazayaanh. Mii maampii ge gwa ndoonjibaa.

3   Maampii, Bkejwanong ezhinkaademigak.

4   Shaagnaashii dash, Walpole Island zhinkaademigad shaagnaashii nikeyaa egiigidod.

5   Ngoding maanda gii-zhiwebad na'aa Jiiwegaanh gii-zhinkaaza nishnaabe.

6   Mekdekonye maampii ngoding gii-bi-zhaa.

7   Mekdekonye, niizh go gii-bi-dchiwag.

8   Gii-bbaa-googsekemi dash go oodi. Gii-bi-nsimi go.

9   Mii nikeyaa zhoonyaans gii-zhi-nokiimi sa go naa.

10   Mii dash iw gaa-zhichgeyaang. Googsekemi.

11   Maa dash oodi gii-ni-dgoshinaang oodi Aazhwaakwaa Jiiwegaanh gaa-ndaad.

12   Gii-giibshe ge. Gii-noondaagonaa shwii go gii-nsaakbidooyaang iw mjikaans. Mjikan maa gii-temigad.

JIIWEGAANH STORY

1   OK, we'll start to speak Anishinaabemowin here. My name is Noodin.

2   When I'm called by my Anishinaabe name. I'm from here.

3   Here, it's called Bkejwanong.

4   In English, though, it's called Walpole Island, in the way it's said in English.

5   Once, this happened: Jiiwegaanh was this man's name in Anishinaabemowin.

6   A priest came here once.

7   Priests, two of them came.

8   We were going around frog hunting over there. There were three of us.

9   That's what we were doing to make some money.

10   Then that's what we did. We hunted frogs.

11   Then we arrived over in backsettlement, where Jiiwegaanh lived.

12   He was deaf too, but he heard us open that little fence. There was a fence there.

13 Gii-noondaan dash mjikan ge, aanii ta gii naa ge-kidayaambaanh. "Biindgen!" gii-kida. Gii-biindgeyaang dash.

14 Mii dash "Aaniish ezhitooyeg maampii?" gii-kida. "ndi-bbaa-googsekemi" ndinaa dash. "oonh enh. Oonh, gii-bbaa-yaawaag sa go ge yaa magakiinsag," kida. Anishinaabe go chi-zhaazhi go mii kaandwewaad.

15 Mii dash maanda gaa-kidad, "Enh, chi-zhaazhi go gwiindmoonim, dbaajmotoonim," kida.

16 "Pii gii-bi-dgoshing maampii Mekdekonye, mii dash iw Bible ezhinikaadeg."

17 Shaagnaashiiwinikaade mii i' gaa-biidood iw. Sii nsaakbidood iw.

18 Webi-gindang dash iw. Mii dash maa naa pane go shpiming gii-zhinooge.

19 "Heaven," kida. "Heaven," kida. Gindang iw Bible ezhinikaadeg.

20 Biibaagi aapta-giizhgak go mii maa go naa Anishinaabeg maa. "Ahaaw, mii sa iw, nii-ni-maajaami," kida.

21 Mekdekonyeg gii-bi-niizhwag gii-ni-maajaa "nga-bi-bskaabii go ge go namaa go naa niizh eko-giizis oodi goojing," kida.

22 Bezhig wa Anishinaabe gii-yaa wii-aankanootwaad go naa.

23 Mii dash gii-bi-bskaabiid. Mii-sh go gii-bi-bskaabiiwaad miinwaa. Niizhing oodi giizis gii-goojing.

24 Gii-dgoshnawaad dash maa ndowaabmaan anishinaaben. Gaawii ngoji waabmaasiin. Biibaagmaan sko naa.

13 But he heard that fence too. How do I say that again? "Come in!" he said. So we went in.

14 Then, "What are you doing here?" he said. So we tell him, "We're getting frogs." "Oh, yeah. Oh, you're all getting those frogs," he said. That's when Anishinaabe climbed up a long time ago.

15 Then he said this, "Yeah, long time ago, I'll tell you all, I'll tell you all a story," he said.

16 "When a priest came here, and the Bible, it's called."

17 It's called in English, that's what he brought. When he opened that.

18 Then he'd start reading it. And he was always pointing up high.

19 "Heaven," he said, "Heaven." When he was reading what is called the Bible.

20 He shouted for a half a day when the Anishinaabe people were there. "OK, that's it, we're leaving," he said.

21 The two priests that came are going to leave. "I'll return in about two months," he said.

22 One Anishinaabe was there to translate.

23 Then he returned. Then they returned again. It was two months.

24 When they arrived here, they looked around for the Anishinaabe people. They didn't see them anywhere. So he shouted for them.

25 "Aapiish yaayeg? Ngii-bskaabiimi! Aapiish yaayeg? Ngii-bskaabiimi!"

26 Gaa gnige gkendaagzisii nishnaabe. Nishnaabe dash oodi gii-kwaandwed wi mtigong.

27 Aapji ekoozid ow mtig. Mii gaa-nji-biibaagid ow Anishinaabe.

28 Mii-sh go maaba bezhig gaa-aankanootwaad naan "pane-sh ge gii-zhinooge ishpiming," kida "'Heaven,' kida, 'Heaven. Mii oodi gaa-zhaayeg. Mii oodi nikeyaa. Ge ni-zhaayeg giishin wii-gyakwiyeg ntaa-namaayin pane go. Mii oodi ge-zhaayeg.'"

29 Mii-sh go gii-mkawaad oodi mekdekonyed. Kina go shpiming oodi. Naabid oodi mekdekonyed gtaamgwiinmoog oodi Anishinaabeg oodi mtigoong gii-kwaandwewaad.

30 Mii maanda, I think ah Jiiwegaanh was 106 [years old] at the time he told us this story. One of the elders.

31 Mii maanda giishenh dbaajmotaadwaad go naa Anishinaabek chi-zhaazhi go.

32 Maanda nikeyaa gaa-zhi-maajiigin, maanda anishinaabemowin aabdeg wii-anishinaabemwaad pane go.

33 Mii go genii gaa-gooyaanh pane go. "Anishinaabemon!"

34 Gaawii wiikaa nda-wnitoosiin ya gii-miin'gooyaanh debenjiged.

35 "Giin gwa, Anishinaabemwin pane shko gdaabjitoon." Mii gaa-gooyaanh iw.

25   "Where are you all? We returned! Where are you all? We returned!"

26   There weren't even any Anishinaabe people there. One Anishinaabe climbed up in the tree.

27   That really tall tree, that's where the Anishinaabe shouted from.

28   Then the one who translates for them, told them, "You were always pointing up high," he said, "'Heaven,' he says, 'Heaven. That's where you all went. In that direction. And you all are going to go there too if you pray all the time.'"

29   Then the priest found them over there. Everyone was up there. As the priest looked over there, there were lots of Anishinaabe people that climbed up [into the trees].

30   Jiiwegaanh was 106 [years old] at the time he told us this story. One of the elders.

31   This is a little bit of what the Anishinaabe people told each other a long time ago.

32   This is how it grew, this Anishinaabemowin. It was necessary for them to speak it all the time.

33   That's what I was always told. "Speak Anishinaabemowin!"

34   I never want to lose what was given to me by the Creator.

35   "You always use Anishinaabemowin." That's what I was told.

GII-ZHAAYAANH *RESIDENTIAL SCHOOL*

1 Ngii-bi-daapnigoo dash ngoding. *Residential School* zhinkaademigad.

2 Mii oodi, ngii-zhiwnigoo oodi. Naan-ndsa-bboon go ngii-ndsa-bboongiz. *Five.*

3 Mii oodi pii genii gii-ni-dgoshinyaanh, oodi mishoo oodi yaa miin'aa bezhig *Indian agent* gii-wiindmowaan aabdeg oodi wii-zhinaashkaagooyaanh. Gii-ni-giiwe dash ngoding miikanaang ge naa ndaapnigoo.

4 Mii dash oodi gaa-zhiwnigooyaanh oodi. Ni-dgoshinayaanh dash oodi gaawii ngkendziin maanda shaagnaashii, shaagnaash, shaagnaashiimwin go naa.

5 Gaawii ngkendziin. Aabdeg kina. Aabdeg ngiikmigoo. Eh, Ba, Ka, Da. Nimosh ge. Gaazhgenh. Bezhgoogzhii. Aabdeg gii-gkinoomaagooyaanh.

6 Ngii-nigaa'goo sko naa. Gegaa go naa eta. Gaa go naa wiya maa gii-yaasii go maa gnoonag. Niin go naa enweyaanh, *Chippewa.*

7 Gaa wiya maa baamaa maa go naa niizh ngoji go giizis wii-ni-dgoshinawaad maa nishnaabensag maampii gii-njibaawag ge wiinwaa.

8 Mii dash maa gaa-ndzhi-nishnaabemyaang.

WHEN I WENT TO RESIDENTIAL SCHOOL

1   So I got picked up one time. Residential School, it's called.

2   Over there, I was brought over there. Five years old, I was. Five.

3   When I arrived over there at that time, my grandfather was there and the Indian agent told him I had to be placed over there. I went home once, but I got picked up on the road.

4   Then I was taken over there. After I arrived there, I didn't know how to speak English.

5   I didn't know anything [about English]. I had to be taught it all: eh, ba, ka, da, and dog, cat, horse. It had to be taught to me.

6   They treated me poorly, almost just me. There was no one there for me to talk to in how I spoke, Chippewa [language].

7   It wasn't until later, about two months, that Anishinaabe kids arrived there from here [Bkejwanong].

8   That is where we began to speak Anishinaabemowin.

9   Dbi go iidig ko waabmagwaa gonda, maazis, aaah *school, and we'd* …
     anishinaabemwaad gonda binoojiinyag gaa-bi-njibaawaad maampii.
     Anishnaabemwaad.

10   Mii-sh go genii gii-nishnaabemyaang ge ni-gkinoomaage
     anishinaabe. Bezhig dash maa shaagnaash endso-gaa …
     Anishinaabemyang gii-oo-zhaa oodi, "Gegwa zhichgeyeg iw,"
     gii-kida.

11   "Gaawii maanda maampii gaa-bi-njibaasiiwag. Aabdeg gwii-
     shaagnaashiim," kida. "Giishin miinwaa maanda zhichgeyeg,
     gwii-pshizhegoo," kida.

12   Mii-sh go miinwaa, miinwaa Anishinaabemying oodi miinwaa.

13   "Gaawii zhichgeyeg iw gwii-pshizhegoo dash." Mii dash mii iw
     gaa-zhiwebak iw. Ninjiing ngii-pshizhegoo ngoding.

14   Gii-*Catch*-migooyaanh wedi maanda nishnaabemying. Niizhing
     dash, "zhichgeyeg maanda." Mii dash niizhing. "Maa ga-pshizhegoo,
     niizhing."

15   Ahaaw, mii-sh go gii-boontaayaanh eshkam go ni-
     waawiisgagnaamigoo sko naa maa ninjiing.

16   Ah, nswi. Nswi sko naa. Mii dash genii eshkam shko gaawii go maa
     ninjiing geyaabi go shpiming oodi, ngii-pshizhegoo.

17   Mii-sh go yaa *part of* wiisginez sko naa. Mii gaa-zhiwebak oodi.

18   Gaa dash miinwaa ngii-nishinaabemsii maa oodi gaa … Mii-sh go eta
     shaagnaashiimyaanh.

19   Ngii-booni-pshizhegoo dash.

9   Whenever I saw them around at school, and we'd ... they would speak Anishinaabemowin, these children that came from here [Bkejwanong]. They spoke Anishinaabemowin.

10 Then when we were also speaking Anishinaabemowin, and we'd teach the language. There was one white man, every time... when we spoke Anishinaabemowin we'd go over there, "Don't do that," he said.

11 "This is not where they're from. You have to speak English." He said. "If you all do it again, then you'll get a strapping," he said.

12 Then again, we were speaking Anishinaabemowin over there.

13 "Don't do that, because you'll get a strapping." Then that's what happened when we talked. I got hit on the hands once.

14 When I got caught over there speaking this language. So the second time, "when you all do this." Then it was twice. "You'll get strapped here [higher on wrist], twice."

15 OK, so then I stopped because it hurt a little more, here on my hands.

16 Ah, three. Third time. Then, not here [pointing at wrists], I got hit higher on my hands here.

17 Then it [part of the wrist] hurt so. That's what happened over there.

18 So I didn't speak Anishinaabemowin again over there. No. So then I just spoke English.

19 Eventually, I was no longer punished.

20   'Di bi-bskaabiiyaanh dash oodi. Gii-bi-giiweyaanh sko naa. Nswi-nsa-
     bboong. Gaawii gii-bi-...endaayaanh sko naa.

21   Mii-sh go, mishoomsag miinwaa mishoo *and* miin'aa *grandma.*
     Mishoo *and* nookmis. Mii-sh go eta gaa-giigidowaad iw
     nishnaabemwag. Mii-sh go genii gii-bi-zhaayaanh maa *holiday
     vacation, two months.*

22   *Then* mii-sh go eta gaa-kidawaad gii-nishinaabemwag. Mii dash genii
     gii-nishnaabemyaanh miin'aa go nootwaag giw Mishoomis miin'aa
     (nookmis).

23   Bskaabiiyaanh dash miinwaa oodi shaagnaashiimyaanh miinwaa.
     Mii-sh go *eight. Eight years.* Bezhig, niizh, nswi, niiwin, naanan... *But I
     lost a lot of my English, and so I talked a little bit right here. A lot of words I can't
     say, but I'm doing the best I can. And that's the way it went with me.* Niin go
     naa. Nishnaabemyaanh.

20 But when I returned over there, when I went home, three years, I didn't ... where I lived.

21 Then, my grandfather and grandma, they only spoke Anishinaabemowin. So when I came back for holiday vacation, two months.

22 Then, that's all they spoke was Anishinaabemowin. Then I spoke Anishinaabemowin again by repeating my grandfather and grandmother.

23 So when I returned over there I spoke English again. Then eight. Eight years. One, two, three, four, five ... But I lost a lot of my English, and so I talked a little bit right here. A lot of words I can't say, but I'm doing the best I can. And that's the way it went with me, as far as I go, when I speak Anishinaabemowin.

NMISHOOMIS MIINWAA NOOKMIS

1   Thomas Isaac gii-zhinkaaza. Waabshkaankwod dash
    nishnaabenikaazad.

2   *And Anna was my grandma.* Nookmis gii-zhinkaaza. Jibwaa wiidged
    dash, *Kiyosh* gii-zhinkaaza. Anna Kiyosh. *Grandma,* mishoomis. Mii
    gwa.

3   Enh, ngii-nishnaabemtowaag gwa. Gii-zhimaagaawi ge gwa maaba
    Thomas, Waabshkaankwod.

4   *World War* I gii-bi-bskaabiid, mii-sh go ge, gewii gii-bi-bskaabii
    nishinaabemad pane miinwaa.

5   *And* gii-bi-bskaabiid powwows gii-bbaa-zhaa. Gii-bbaa-dewege.
    Gii-ngamo ge gwa.

6   Dewegan pane gwa miin'aa ko ngoji. Nswi go gii-zhitoonan Teepees
    ezhinikaadeg. Wiib.

7   Gii-aabjitoonaawaan mtig. Wiib. Gii-zhitoowaad. Gii-
    binoojiinswiyaanh go naa ngii-noondwaag oodi ngamwaad
    dewe'igewaad oodi endaayaang.

8   Ngii-zhaa ko oodi. Gii-mnataagziwag sa dewe'igewaad, ngamwaad.

9   Mii-sh gaa-…gii-gkendaanaawaa sko naa moozhaan…ngii-
    moozh'ig sko naa.

GRANDFATHER AND GRANDMOTHER

1   Thomas Isaac was his name, Waabshkaankwod when he was called his Anishinaabe name.

2   And Anna was my grandma, my grandma's name. Before she got married, Kiyosh was her name, Anna Kiyosh. Grandma, grandfather.

3   Yeah, I spoke Anishinaabemowin to them. He was a soldier too, Thomas, Waabshkaankwod.

4   World War I he returned from. Then, he returned to speaking Anishinaabemowin all the time again.

5   And when he returned, he went to powwows. He went around drumming. He sang too.

6   He was always drumming again everywhere. He made three teepees. Elm tree

7   They used a tree, an elm tree. They made it. When I was a boy, I heard them over there singing and drumming over at our house.

8   I use to go over there. They sounded good when they drummed and sang.

9   Then … they knew when they felt it … they felt my presence.

10   Nengaach widi ezhi-…gii-zhaayaanh oo-dzhi edzhi-ngamwaad.

11   Gii-biibaagid go naa Tom. "Go on home!" kida. "Ni-giiwen! Bibaa-zhitooyin maampii?" Giiweyaanh ko. Mii maanda gaa-zhichgewaad ko.

12   Zhimaagaanyik gaa-bskaabiiwaad oodi World War I. Nishnaabeg. I think there was Joe, Joe Tooshkenig. Zhaawanoo gii-zhinkaaza. And Elijah Isaac. Elijah Sword gii-zhinkaaza bezhig. And sayenyan Elijah. Thomas Isaac. Sayenyan. His brother. Mii ow gaa-zhichgewaad.

10   Quietly [snuck]...when I went over there over there where they sang.

11   Tom would yell. "Go on home!" he said. "Go home! What are you doing here?" I use to go home. This is what they use to do.

12   The soldiers that returned from over there World War I. Anishinaabe men. I think there was Joe, Joe Tooshkenig. 'Zhaawanoo' was his [Anishinaabe] name. And Elijah Isaac. Elijah Sword was that one's name. And his older brother, Thomas Isaac. His older brother. His brother. That's what they did.

GAA MNA-MINIK ZHOONYAA GII-MIIJGAAZSIIWAG

1 Miin'aa ko ngoji gii-bbaa-zhaawag *powwows* zhinkaademigad.

2 Gii-zhaawaad ko oodi, gii-bbaa-ngamwaad gii-dewe'igewaad gaa-paa-niimwaad.

3 Maanda dash ngoding 'Papa,' ngii-naa ko, Thomas, mishoo. 'Papa' ngii-naa.

4 Ngii-wiindmaag ngoding. Gaawii mna-minik zhoonyaa gii-miizhgaazsiiwag.

5 "Nii-boontaami" kida. "Gaa mna-minik zhoonyaa ndo-miinigoosiimi" Gwegwendig dash maa niigaanzid zhaagnaash. "Gegwa zhichigeke go iw."

6 Nshkaadziitaadoog go naa. Mii-sh go naa "ahaaw! Miizhyaang iw zhoonyaa. Nii-niimi maampii wii-gchi-gmiwang," kida. "*Rain dance* nga-zhitoonaa, wii-gchi-gmiwang dash."

7 Gii-waabdamwaad go naa nishinaabeg bi-ngwaankwad go naa oodi. Dewe'igewaad, gchi-ngamwag. Mii-sh go ge gaa-zhiwebak iw. Ngwaankwak, gchi-gmiwan, chi-nimkiikaamigad ge gwa.

8 Mii dash maa eyaawaad gii-gchi-noodin ge go.

9 Kina gegoo miin'aa ngoji aaboodaasinwag gchi-*tent* gii-aabjitoonaa gchi-wiigwaam go naa gii-aaboodaasing yaa.

THEY WEREN'T GIVEN ENOUGH MONEY

1   And they use to go around to powwows, as they're called elsewhere.

2   They'd go there, go around singing and drumming and dancing.

3   So this one time Papa, I use to call him that, Thomas, my grandfather. Papa I called him.

4   He told me this once. They weren't given enough money.

5   "We were going to quit," he said. "We weren't given the right amount of money." I don't know who this white guy was; the boss was a white guy. "Don't do that."

6   They were arguing [mad at one another]. Then "OK! Give us that money. We'll dance here to make it rain hard," he said. "We'll make a rain dance, to make a rain storm then."

7   The Anishinaabe saw it begin to get cloudy over there. They drummed and sang hard. Then it happened. It got cloudy and rained hard, thunderstormed too.

8   Then it came there; it was really windy too.

9   Everything and everywhere was blowing over. A big tent that they used as a big house was flipped over by the wind there.

10 Geget maa niigaanzid ow shaagnaash "Gegwa zhichgeken! Boontaag! Boontaag!" kida. *That's 'stop.'* "Ahaaw! Ga-miinin go zhoonyaa!" kida.

11 Mii-sh go mii maa naa go dbaajmotaadiwaad.

12 Giishenh naa, nmishoo. Mii maanda gaa-kidad.

13 Dbaajmotaadiyaang go naa. Mii maanda gaa-zhiwebak oodi zhaagnaashii-kiing go naa. *Ohio,* zhinkaademigad oodi gaa-zhiwebak oodi.

14 Ah mii sa. Giishenh go naa gaa-zhiwebak Anishinaabeg oodi. Brown ge gwa zhinkaazad zhaagnaash. Mr. Brown gii-zhinkaanaawaan. Mii-sh go gii-gshkitoowaad iw zhoonyaa. Gii-bi-gtaamgwok.

10 The leader, the white man, "Don't do that! Stop! Stop!" he says. That's "stop." "OK! I'll give you the money!" he said.

11 So that's the stories they told each other.

12 A little bit, my grandfather, this is what he said.

13 When we told stories to each other, this is what happened over there in United States. Ohio, it's called, it happened over there.

14 Ah that's it. A little bit of what happened to the Anishinaabe people over there. Brown, that was the white man's name. Mr. Brown they called him. Then they were able to get their money, when the storm came.

GAA-ZHITOOWAAD

1   Gchi-zhaazhi go ge gwa. Gii-gokbinaaganikewag gonda kwewag
miinwaa zhebii'aanan gii-zhitoonaawaan. *And hammer. Had a*
wepjigan.

2   (Jennie Blackbird) 'Wepjigaansan.'

3   Enh mii iw. Wepjigaansan gii-zhitoonaawaan pii bbaa-daawewaad
ko. Shkode-naapkowaanan ko gii-bmibdenoon maampii ziibiing.

4   Oodi Waawyejwang nikeyaa gii-zhaawag ko Anishinaabeg.

5   Jiimaanan oodi gii-aabjitoonaawaan. Gokbinaagaans, zhebii'aanan,
wepjigaansan gii-booztoonaawaa maa jiimaanensan.

6   Mii dash pii shkode-naapkowaan maa gii-bmibdeg. Sabaabiins oodi
gii-pagdoonaawaa ko oodi.

7   Gonda bembideg. Shkode-naapkowaaning enokiijig. Sabaabiins
gii-pagdoonaawaa. Anishinaabe dash gii-aabjitoonaawaa iw.

8   Mii dash oodi gii-zhaawaad oodi. *Detroit,* Waawyejiwang. Chi-waasa
ge ko oodi Wiikwemikong ko gii-zhaawag.

9   Oodi nikeyaa gii-bbaa-daawewaad. Gwegwendig ko gaa-zhitoowaad.

10 Mii dash ji-jaagdaawewaad, mii dash ji-bi-bskaabiiwaad
baabiitoowaad.

WHAT THEY MADE

1   A long time ago too, these women made baskets and they made oars. And hammer. Had a hammer.

2   (Jennie Blackbird) Wepjigaansan.

3   Yeah, that's it. They use to make hammers, and they went around selling them. Steamboats use to go along here on the river.

4   The Anishinaabe people use to go over there toward Detroit.

5   They used boats over there. They uploaded baskets, oars, hammers there on the little boats.

6   Then at that time the steamboats ran there. They use to throw a rope over there.

7   These ones that ride along, the workers on the steamboats, they'd throw the rope. Anishinaabe people used that.

8   Then they went over there, Detroit, Waawyejiwang. They also use to go really far over to Wiikwemikong.

9   They went around selling over there, whatever they use to make.

10 Then when they sold everything, they returned and waited [for the boat].

11 Mii dash maampii nikeyaa wii-bi-giiwewaad. Mii-sh go miin'aa gaa-zhichgewaad sabaabiins oodi gii-pagdoonaawaa.

12 Mii dash gii-bi-bskaabiiwaad maampii mnisheying mii maanda gaa-zhi-bbaa-daawewaad Nishnaabeg chi-zhaazhi go naa.

13 Shkode-naapkowaanan gii-zhinkaadenoon *steamboats*. Chi-zhaazhi go go naa iw.

14 Mii dash nikeyaa gii-zhoonyaakewaad giw Nishnaabeg maampii. Weweni dash wii-ni-maajiwaad niigaan nikeyaa. Daawegamigoon ge gwa gii-tenoon maa mnisheying.

15 Aazhwaakwaa bezhig gii-temigad miin'aa.

16 Jiigbiing, jiigbiing gii-zhinkaademigad maampii bezhig. Mii eta miin'aa bezhig Potawatomi nikeyaa.

17 *Potawatomi Island* gii-zhinkaademigad oodi bezhig. Enh, mii iw gaa-zhoonyaakenswiwaad *bittersweet*. Gii-bbaa-daawewaad ko miin'aa *sweetgrass*. Wiingashk.

18 Potholders gii-zhitoowaad, gii-zhitoowaad ko kwewag miin'aa *baskets. Sweetgrass baskets, they use to take*. Wiingashk go naa. Mii maanda gaa-zhi-, nikeyaa, gaa-zhi-zhoonyaakenswiwaad gonda maampii eyaajig.

19 Eshkam-sh go naa gaa'ii tesnoo maampii. Iw nikeyaa.

20 Gaa wiya yaasii maampii dash ezhitood niw gokbinaagaansan.

21 Mii maanda ezhi-nikeyaa, ezhi-nigaaziyaang.

22 Gaa go naa wiya yaasii noongo naa, yaasii waa-zhitood gokbinaaganan kina go nikeyaa.

11 Then they'd come home here this way. Then again they'd do that with the rope over there. They'd throw it.

12 Then they'd return here to the island from going around selling to the Anishinaabe people, a long time ago.

13 Shkode-naapkowaanan is what they called steamboats, a long time ago that is.

14 So that's the way they made money, those Anishinaabe people here. They were careful to take it into the future. There were stores here on the island.

15 There was one in backsettlement too.

16 At the beach, the beach [up front] one was called here. And only another one toward Potawatomi.

17 Potawatomi Island one was called over there. Yeah, that's what they made money with, bittersweet, they use to go around selling and sweetgrass. Wiingashk.

18 They made potholders. The women use to make baskets. Sweetgrass baskets, they use to take. Sweetgrass. This is the way they made a little bit of money here, the ones who were here.

19 More and more that way is not here anymore, that way [of living].

20 No one is here to make those baskets.

21 This is the way we are poor.

22 No one here today, no one wants to make baskets in all those ways.

23 *Sweetgrass baskets*, kina go. Kondiinsan, gwegwendig go. Wepjigaansan ge go.

24 Zhebii'aanan gaa'ii go wiya zhitoosiin iw maampii dash. Mii iw nikeyaa ezhi-nigaaziyaang maampii.

25 Kina go ezhi-...maampii ezhitoowaad. Gchi-gaaming oodi, *China*. Kina go wa maampii eyaabjitooyaang.

26 *Made in China*. Mii oodi zhinkaademigak iw. Mii oodi ezhitoowaad oodi. Maampii dash mii go geniin maampii eyaabjitooyaang. Ezhi-nigaaziyaang iw nikeyaa.

27 Mbegish naa, niin go naa. Enendmaanh. Mbegish bskaabiimgak iw maanda ko gaa-zhichgeyaang.

28 Mii maanda ezhi-nigaaziyaang. Giishenh iw nikeyaa gaa-zhi-wiindmoonnaa.

29 Gchi-waasa ko genii ndoo-bbaa-zhaa gaa-zhichgewaad oodi pane go ndakwejimaag "Aaniish ezhi-zhoonyaakeyeg maampii?"

30 Mii-sh go naa naasaab oodi ezhiwebak oodi bbaa-zhaayaanh bi-mbwaachweyaanh go naa Nishnaabeg.

31 Giiwednong, zhaawnong ge gwa oodi. Mii go naasaab ge ezhiyaawaad oodi.

32 Aabdeg nokii shaagnaashiikiing aabdeg wii-oo-nokii zhoonyaans wii-gshkitoowaad wii-bmaadziwaad maampii.

33 Enh mii-sh ga. Mii sa iw nikeyaa ge gaa-dbaajmotaadiyaang giishenh.

23   Sweetgrass baskets, everything, basket handles, whatever. Hammers as well.

24   Oars, too, no one makes that here anymore. That's how poor we are here.

25   Everything here they made across the ocean, China. Everything that we use here.

26   Made in China, that's what it's called over there. They make it over there. We use it here too. That's how we are poor.

27   As for me, I hope. What I think. I hope this comes back, what we use to do.

28   This is how we're poor. A little bit of that way, what I told you.

29   Me, I use to go a long ways to where they did it. I always ask them, "How are you making money here?"

30   And the same thing is happening over there when I go around over there visiting Anishinaabe people.

31   Up north, over there in the south too, they are also living the same way there.

32   One has to work hard in the white world to be able to live here.

33   Yeah, that's it. That's a little bit of the way we tell stories.

Naawkwe-giizhgo-kwe

Reta Sands gii-dbaajma / Stories told by Reta Sands

EYAAWIYAANH

1   Naawkwe-giizhgo-kwe ndizhnikaaz.

2   Pottawaatomie Island ngii-zhi-ndaadiz.

3   Pane go naa Ojibwe ngii-kid ezhi-giigidayaanh.

4   Mii shwii gwa ezhi-gkendmaanh noongwa Odawa nda-zhi-giigid.

5   Giishenh gaye Podewaadmi ngii-gkendaan gaa-zhi-noondmaanh
bi-kognigooyaanh.

6   Mii go gnabaj iw kina.

7   {Geyaabi na niibna boodewaadimiig maampii?}

8   Gaawii ganabaj aapji boodewaadmiig yaasiiwag.

9   Mii gonaa genealogy gaa-zhichged Sylvia Deleary miinwaa Suzie
Jones miinwaa Linda White.

10   The last Monday of each month, gii-maawnjitoonaawaa genealogy.

11   Niizh giizhgadoon gii-waabdowewag oodi Band office,
'Naaknigegamigoong' gaa-zhinkamwaad.

12   Mii-sh ko aanind nishnaabeg gii-waabadamwaad, gaa-zhi-
ndaadziwaad giw Potowaadimiiyag nikeyaa. Gaa shwii go kina,
aanind go eta.

WHO I AM

1   My name is Naawkwe-giizhgo-kwe.

2   Potawatomi Island is where I was born.

3   I always said I spoke Ojibwe.

4   But today I know it as Odawa.

5   I knew a little bit of Potawatomi language, as I heard it as I was being raised.

6   That's about all of it.

7   {Is there still a lot of Potawatomi people here?}

8   There's not really a lot of Potawatomi people.

9   Sylvia Deleary does that genealogy along with Suzie Jones and Linda White.

10   The last Monday of each month, they gather it over there, genealogy.

11   Two days they show it over at the Band office, Naaknigegamigoong, they named it.

12   Some Anishinaabe people got to see that they were born over on Potawatomi Island. But not everyone, just some.

GAA-ZHI-GOKBINAAGANIKEWAAD MEWNZHA

1 Pii gii-gaashiin'iyaanh, mii go eta gaa-zhichgewaad gchi-kizheb.
Ninwag baagaakogewaad.

2 Ntam gwegwendig iidig waa-gshkozgwenh.

3 Mii go gii-zaasaakwed, mii go ge'e giw aanind ninwag gii-ni-
zaasaakwewaad. Mii dash miinwaa gii-webi-baagaakogewaad
chi-kizheb jibwaa gzhideg.

4 Mii dash gewiinwaa kwewag gii-naagzhigewaad niw baagaakoganan
miinwaa gii-biiszhwaawaad, miinwaa gii-tiswaawaad.

5 Mii dash owedi miishkokoong gii-pagnaawaad gii-shkwaa-
tiswaawaad. Mii dash gii-aabji'aawaad gokbinaaganikewaad
maagnigewaad nooj go iw nikeyaa.

6 Nooj gegoo gii-zhitoonaawaa niw dnowan gokbinaaganan.

7 Mii dash mna-minik gshkapjiganan minik gii-mi-zhitoowaad mii
gii-zhiwdoonaawaa owedi chi-mookmaankiing, gii-o-daawewaad.

8 Mii-sh ko wiigwaam miinwaa wiigwaam gii-zhaawaad, gii-
kwedwewaad giishpin endowendmowaagwenh giw shagnaashag
gokbinaaganan.

9 Mii-sh ko gii-daawewaad.

10 Pii gii-jaagdaawewaad mii dash miijim gii-o-giishnadoowaad.

HOW THEY MADE BASKETS LONG AGO

1   When I was small, that's all they did early in the morning. The men pounded wood [to make basket splints].

2   Whoever the first one would be to wake up.

3   Then holler in joy, that's when some of those men whooped up too. Then they'd start pounding the wood again early in the morning before it got hot.

4   Then the women would scrape the splints, they would cut them into pieces, and then they would dye the splints.

5   Then they'd throw the splints in the grass once they dyed them. Then they'd use them when they were making the baskets and weave them in various ways.

6   They'd make different kinds of those baskets.

7   Then when they made enough packages, they'd take them over to the United States and sold them.

8   They use to go to house to house, and they'd ask the white people if they needed baskets.

9   They use to sell them.

10 When they sold out, they'd go buy food.

11   Mii dash giiwewdoowaad kina wiya dash gii-ni-wiisini minik gaa-
     biidoowaad giw kwewag. Mii iw gaa-zhiwebak ko.

12   {Kii daawe?}

13   Enh.

14   {Aapiish?}

15   Chi-mookmaanking Algonac, Marine City, toward Port Huron.

16   Mii genii gaa-ko-zhaayaanh. Nookmis shwii gwa, nooj go naa
     gii-zhaadig.

17   {Aaniish ezhnikaazad?}

18   Irene Armstrong. Nookmisba.

19   {Gii-nitaa-gokbinaaganikeba?}

20   Enh, aapji gwa gii-mshkozii maa ninjiin.

21   Gdaa-waabmaa gonaa gaa-piichi-mzhkoziid maa ninjiin.

22   Niw emchaagin gokbinaaganan mii niw dnowan gaa-zhitoojin.

23   Hampers miinwaa gwiiwnan wii-toong. Gnooyaanoon go niw,
     mchaanoon niw, laundry baskets.

24   Gii-mngadeyaanoon miinwaa gii-gnooyaanoon mii niw dnowan
     gaa-zhitoojin miinwaa market baskets mii niw dnowan gaa-zhitoojin.

25   Mechaagin gwa gokbinaaganan gii-zhitoonan.

26   Niw dash dawemaan Eva gii-zhinkaazwan.

11 Those women brought the food home so everyone could eat. That's what use to happen.

12 {Did you sell them?}

13 Yes.

14 {Where?}

15 In the United States, Algonac, Marine City, toward Port Huron.

16 That's as far as I went. But my late grandmother, she must've gone to various other places.

17 {What is her name?}

18 Irene Armstrong, my grandmother [since passed].

19 {Was she good at basketmaking?}

20 Yeah, she had really strong hands.

21 You could see how strong her hands were.

22 Those big baskets, that's the kind she made.

23 Hampers to put clothes in. Long ones, big ones, laundry baskets.

24 They were wide and long, the kind she made. And market baskets, that's the kind she made.

25 She made the big baskets.

26 So her sister's name was Eva.

27 Mii gewii ow gaa-jejenj-gokbinaaganiked.

28 Aapji gwa gii-gaashnoonini niw jejenj-gokbinaaganan gaa-zhitoojin
Eva.

29 Gaawii gii-mmaangninjiisii, gechwaa naa niin nookomis. Gii-
gaachninjii Eva.

30 Gnaajwani gaa-zhitoojin. Jejenji'iin.

31 {Noongwa dash gwis gii-zhitood.}

32 Ngwis gii-waabdaan iw chi-gokbinaagan oodi daabaanag gii-biwaad
jiigi-wiigwaaming.

33 Gete'ii gonaa gokbinaaganan nookmisba gaa-zhitood. Mii dash
gii-wiindmowag minik gaa-zhi-ntaa-nakiid gchi-nookmisan.

34 Mii dash iidig gii-mnjimendang. Mii dash gii-noondang owedi
jiigi-gkinoomaagewgamigoong Marie miinwaa Levina wii-
gkinoomaagewaad.

35 Mii-sh ko gii-o-zhaad gewii oodi gii-o-gkinoomaagzid.

36 Miinwaa oodi chi-mookmaankiing gii-noondang *weekend workshop*.

37 Mii-sh ko ge'ii oodi gii-pizad, miinwaa nwanj gii-gkendang waa-zhi-
gokbinaaganiked.

38 Miinwaa pii gii-bi-giiwed gii-miizhgaaza aanind baagaakoganan.

39 Mii-sh ko ge'ii maampii Bkejwanong gii-zhitood nooj gegoo
gokbinaaganan.

27   She was a fancy basket maker too.

28   Eva made really small fancy baskets.

29   She didn't have big hands like my grandmother. Eva had small hands.

30   They were beautiful baskets that she made. They were fancy.

31   {But now your son makes them.}

32   My son saw that big basket over there by the cars that were beside the house.

33   Old baskets my grandmother had made. Then I told him how much amazing work his great-grandmother did.

34   So he probably he remembered. Then he heard about when Marie and Levina were going to teach at the school.

35   So he would go over there to learn.

36   And in the States, he heard about a weekend workshop.

37   So he drove over there too and learned more of how to make baskets.

38   And again he came home and was given some splints.

39   Then he began to make various kinds of baskets here in Bkejwanong.

40   Mii-sh go pane go bi-daawed *Potawaadimi* Gathering gii-zhiwdoonan
gokbinaaganan gaa-zhitoojin. Gii-waabdaanaawaa giw *Potawaadimiig*.
Mii-sh go ngodooshkin iw mkak minik gokbinaaganan gaa-teg
maa doopwining gii-yaawaanaa … gii-yaa giw Potawaadimiig gii-
giishnadoonaawaa.

41   Mii shko eta niizh gii-shkoseg. Ngii-wiindmowaa shko gaa-piichi-
maamiikwaabdamwaad giw gaa-bi-zhaajig.

42   Mii shko eta gii-zhooshmiingwenid.

43   Niiwaak minik zhoonyaa gii-gshkitoon iw pii gii-bi-zhaawaad giw
Potawaadimiig.

44   Gii-maamiikwendam shko. Miinwaa gii-gkendaan waa-zhi-
gokbinaaganiked.

45   Gaa dash gegoo iw waa-aabjitood diyaanziin.

46   Gaa shko maamdaa, gaawii noongwa wiisgaak yaasii maa
Bkejwanong. Giisaadkamik gwa.

40   Then when he came to sell at the Potowaadimi Gathering, he brought the baskets that he made. The Potawatomi saw them. Then one bagful, as much in a box, of the baskets were on the table were … all bought up by those Potawatomi people.

41   There were only two leftover. I told him how amazed they were at what they saw by the attendees.

42   He just smiled.

43   He was able to make $400 when the Potawatomi came.

44   He was happy. And he knew how to make baskets.

45   But there's nothing for him to use.

46   He can't, there are no black ash trees here in Bkejwanong today. It's sad.

GAA-WEBI-GKINOOMAAGEYAANH

1 Ngoji gonaa 1963, ngii-bbaa-yaanaaba Woodstock.

2 Mii dash gii-waabdamaanh *advertising* maa Bkejwanong ndowenjgaazad egkinoomaaged.

3 Mii dash gii-kwejtooyaanh nakiiwin wii-yaamaanh, mii shko gii-gshkitooyaanh.

4 Gii-bi-giiweyaanh, mii dash iw pii gaa-webi-gkinooomaageyaanh, 1963.

5 Mii dash ngoji 1977 gii-ndowenjgaazad enishnaabemad wii-gkinoomaaged.

6 Gii-ni-gkendaanaawaa go naa niw ni-chigaadeg iw nishnaabemowin, mii dash maanda gaa-nji-kidwaad.

7 Gaa go naa debsesnoo giw getzijig ekdowaad.

8 Gaa gonaa aapji bzindaajgaazsiiwag. Ga-wnitoonaa maanda nishnaabemowin giishpin gonda binoojiinyag bwaa-noondmowaad.

9 Mii dash gii-webtaayaanh naan'godnong gwa *kindergarten* naazh gwa *grade* nswi.

10 *Rotary* ngii-gkinoomaage. Miinwaa ngoding *interim* ngii-gkinoomaage.

WHEN I STARTED TEACHING

1   About 1963, I had been living around over there in Woodstock.

2   Then I saw an advertising here that a teacher was needed here in Bkejwanong.

3   So I tried to get the job, and I was able to get it.

4   When I came home, that is when I started teaching, in 1963.

5   Then about 1977, they needed an Anishinaabemowin speaker to teach.

6   They started to realize the language was being lost, and that's why they said this.

7   There were not enough elders who spoke the language.

8   No one really listens to them. We'll lose this Anishinaabemowin if these children don't hear it.

9   Then I started occasionally at kindergarten through grade three.

10   Rotary, I taught. Also, I once taught interim.

11   Miinwaa *senior* ngii-gkinoomaage. Gaawii go eta bezhigonong gwa dsa-bboon nwanj gwa.

12   Miinwaa ngoding giw eznagzijig wii-gindaaswaad gii-gkinoomowaag kizheb miinwaa nishnaabemwin giw aanind ngii-gkinoomowaag.

13   Mii gaa-zhichgeyaanh oodi gkinoomaagewgamigong.

14   Ngoji gonaa 1995 gnabaj ngii-boontaa oodi gkinoomaageyaanh.

15   {Geyaabi na ggkinoomaage oodi Nimkii-wiiwkwedong?}

16   Niizh dsa-bboon ngoji, gaawii Nimkii-wiiwkwedong ndo-zhaasii.

17   Ngii-waabmaaba Bruce Beardy oodi *Sault Ste. Marie*.

18   Mii gaa-nendmaanh geyaabi oodi niigaanzid. Gaa shwii gewii, bkaan go naa zhi-gkinoomaage.

19   *Long Lac* gnabaj gii-kida.

20   Gaa-sh go gwech gwa ngii-gkendziin ezhchigewaagwenh oodi Nimkii-wiiwkwedong noongwa.

21   Geyaabi go naa gnamaa nswi dsa-bboon, aabdeg … niibnong, aabdeg gwii-zhaanaadig owedi wii-zhaabshkaman maage gwa niiwin gnamaa.

22   Aabdeg go naa wiya da-zhi-giigida oodi maage da-zhi-zhibiige geget go naa wii-gkendming.

11 I also taught senior. Not just one year, but more.

12 And once, those troublesome ones I taught to read in the morning, and I taught some of them Anishinaabemowin.

13 That's what I did over there at the school.

14 Around 1995 maybe, I stopped teaching over there.

15 {Do you still teach over there in Thunder Bay?}

16 For about two years, I haven't gone to Thunder Bay.

17 I had seen Bruce Beardy over there in Sault Ste. Marie.

18 I had thought he was still the director over there, but he's not. He's teaching somewhere different.

19 He might have said in Long Lac.

20 I don't quite know what they're doing in Thunder Bay now.

21 Maybe it's still three years, have to ... during the summer, you might have to go there to graduate, maybe four years.

22 One will really know how to talk and how to write over there.

BWAAJGENG MKADEKENG

1   Mewnzha, gechwaa naa noongwa geyaabi ezhiyaag, gwiiwzens pii dbishkoosenig pii mtigwaakiing wii-zhaad, wii-baabiitoong bwaajgewin.

2   Aabdeg gii-zhitoon wiigwaamens miinwaa gaa gegoo biidoosiin miijim nwezh gii-bgosendam wii-mbwaachigaazad niw wesiinyan maage mnidoon maa mtigwaakiing ebi-njibaanjin wii-zhawenmigod, wii-miingod waa-zhichged miinwaa mshkoziiwin.

3   Gwiiwzens gii-yaa Pichi gii-zhinkaaza gaa-debnang maanda dsa-bboongizwin mdaaswi-zhi-niizh.

4   Pichi oosan gii-gchi-piitendaagziwan maa yaawaad miinwaa gii-nendam ogwisan wii-bwaajgenid iw bwaajgewin iw mshkoziiwin miinwaa gaawii wiya gaa-zhichgesig. Gii-wewiibendmoon oosan, niw gwisan wii-debnamnid mshkoziiwin, mii gaa-kidad gwiiwzensman wii-bwaajgeng mkadekenid jibwaa shkwaaj goonkaag, aanind gwiiwzensag aabdeg baabiichgewag naazh go pii iw ki gzhideg miinwaa niibiishan bskaabiimigak mtigong.

5   "Ngwis mshkozii," kida niw oosan. "Da-maajaa sa. Nwanj da mshkozii iw gsinaamigadnig."

6   Pichi, gwiiwzens gii-aawi, pane gaa-bzindwaad gitziiman mii dash gaa-zhichged oosan gaa-kidnid.

7   Neniizh gii-zhaawag mtigwaakiin miinwaa da-noosman gii-ndowaabdamnid wii-yaad giji aazhbikoonsing.

THE DREAM FAST

1   Long ago, as it still is today, it was the custom for a boy who reached a certain age to go into the forest and wait for a dream.

2   He would build a small lodge and go without food for many days in the hope he would be visited by some animal or spirit of the forest that would take pity on him and give guidance and power.

3   There was a boy named Opichi who reached that age of twelve years old.

4   Opichi's father was very respected in the village, and he was determined that his son would be given a dream of such power that no one else could compare with him. So eager was the father for his son to get power that he insisted the boy go on his dream fast before the last snow left the ground, even though most boys would wait until the time when the ground was warm and the leaves returned to the trees.

5   "My son is strong," said the father. "He will go now. He will gain greater strength from the cold."

6   Opichi was a boy who always wished to please his parents, and so he did as his father said.

7   They went together into the forest, and the father selected a spot on top of a small hill.

8   Mii maa Pichi gii-zhitood mtigwan-wiigwaamens, ezhi-
      maawndoonming tikwaansan naama'iing gii-nmadbi zhashkiin ge
      waawaashkeshi-biiwyan dinmaagning.

9   "Nga-bi-bskaabii nso-giizhig pii biidaabang," gii-kidwan oosan.
      "Ga-wiindmáw dash iw pii gaa-waabdaman."

10   Pii dibikak, gii-wenda-noodin, mkomii-nesewin ow gchi-mko,
      gii-gsinaamgad. Pichi gashwan gii-bookenmoon, gaa sa wii go oosan.
      "Ngwis mshkozii," gii-kida. "Maanda dkeyaag noodin dash nwanj
      da-giiyakwaabi."

11   Pii kizhebaawang gii-zhaa oodi gaa-zhitood miinwaa migwebnang
      mtigoon. "Ngwis," gii-kida, "wiindmoshin gaa-waabdaman."

12   Opichi gii-zaagdoode miinwaa gii-gnowaabmaad oosan. "Noos,"
      gwiiwzens kida, "waawaashkeshi besha gii-bi-zhaa wiigwaaming
      miinwaa gii-bi-gnoonig."

13   "Giiyakwan iw," kidwan oosan. "Aabdeg-sh wii gwa geyaabi ga-
      mkadeke. Geget nwanj e-giiyakwang bwaajgewin ga-debnaan."

14   "Geyaabi nga-ndowaab, miinwaa nga-baabiichge," Opichi gii-kida.

15   Opichi oosan gii-njiknigoon mii dash gii-bskaabiid wiigwaamensing.
      Pii dibikak goonens gii-bngishin.

16   "Ngiisaadendam gwisnaa," kidwan Opichi gashwan. "Gaawii
      giisaadengen," kidwan oosan. "Niw goonan da-naadmaagoon pii
      bwaajged nwanj nda-mshkozii."

17   Pii bmi-waabang, oosan miinwaa mtigwaakiing gii-zhaawan,
      gii-kwaandwed maa aazhbikoonsing miinwaa gii-maamaajwebnang
      niw mtigoonsan miinwaa zaagwewemaad da-gwisman.

8   There, Opichi made a small lean-to of saplings, covering it with hemlock boughs, and he sat beneath it on the bare ground with a thin piece of deerskin wrapped about his shoulders.

9   "I will return each day at dawn," the father said. "You will tell me then what you have seen."

10   That night the north wind, the icy breath of the Great Bear, blew cold. Opichi's mother was concerned, but the father did not worry. "My son is strong," he said. "This cold wind will make his vision a better one."

11   When the morning came, he went to the lean-to and shook the poles. "My son," he said, "tell me what you have seen."

12   Opichi crawled out and looked up at his father. "Father," the boy said, "a deer came to the lodge and spoke to me."

13   "That is good," said the father. "But you must continue to fast. Surely a greater vision will come to you."

14   "I will continue to watch and wait," Opichi said.

15   Opichi's father left his son and went back to his lodge. That night a light snow fell.

16   "I'm worried about our son," said Opichi's mother. "Do not worry," said the father. "The snow will only make whatever dream comes to him more powerful."

17   When morning came, the father went into the forest again, climbed the hill and shook the poles, calling his son out.

18 "Noos," Opichi gii-kida, pii bmi-zaagdooded, aapji ge gii-biingeji,
    "dibikong amik ngii-bi-naashkaag. Ngii-gkinoomaag bezhig
    ngamwin."

19 "Gii-gyakwan iw," kida oosan. "Gda-mnachge. Nwanj mshkoziiwan
    ga-debnaan giishpin yiyaayin."

20 "Nga-kowaabjige miinwaa nga-baabiichge," gii-kida gwiiwzens.

21 Mii sa zhiwebak niiwin minik giizhgadoon. Endsa-kizhebaawgak
    oosan Opichi gii-bi-kwejmigoon gwegwendig gaa-waabangwenh.

22 Endsa-kwejmigaazad gwiiwzens, gii-dbaajdaanan gaa-zhiwebzid,
    gii-dibikadnig. Mii sa gekek, ma'iingan, mko miinwaa migizi gii-
    mbwaach'aawaad gwiiwzensan.

23 Endsa-giizhgak Pichi eshkam gii-ni-gwaakdaza miinwaa
    nwanj gii-bejiiwii, mii sa wii go gii-debwetowaad oosan wii
    yiyaad wii-baabiitoong nwanj emshkoziimgak waabdawin wii-
    gyakwenmigwod oosan.

24 Kizhebaawgak, niizhwaaswi giizhgadoon, Pichi gashwan
    gii-giigdanid, gii-naad naabeman, "Gda-gwisnaa mna-minik
    baabiichge maa mtigwaakiing, ga-wiijiiwin noongwa kizheb ga-bi-
    giiwewnaanaa dash."

25 Pichi gashwan miinwaa oosan neniizh mtigwaakiing gii-zhaawaad.

26 Ezhi-nesed ow gdagaakoons, egzhideg zhaawnong mnookmi-
    noodin, gii-boodaajgemigad dibikak miinwaa kina goon gii-ngiza.

27 Pii kwaandwewaad aazhbikoonsing, gii-noondaanaawaa bineshii-
    ngamwin shpiming nike'iing yaawaad.

28 Iw dnowa ngamwin gaa wiikaa gii-noondziinaawaa. Gechwaa naa
    gwiswaan noozwin gaa-noondmowaad. Pi chi chi.

18 "Father," Opichi said as he emerged, shaking from the cold, "last night a beaver came to me. He taught me a song."

19 "That is good," said the father. "You are doing well. You will gain even more power if you stay longer."

20 "I will watch and wait," said the boy.

21 So it went for four more days. Each morning his father asked Opichi what he had seen.

22 Each time the boy told of his experiences from the night before. Now hawk and wolf, bear and eagle had visited the boy.

23 Each day Opichi looked thinner and weaker, but he agreed to stay and wait for an ever-greater vision to please his father.

24 At last, on the morning of the seventh day, Opichi's mother spoke to her husband. "Our son has waited long enough in the forest. I will go with you this morning and we will bring him home."

25 Opichi's mother and father went together into the forest.

26 The gentle breath of the Fawn, the warm south wind of spring, had blown during the night and all the snow had melted away.

27 As they climbed the hill, they heard a birdsong coming from above them.

28 It was a song they had never heard before. It sounded almost like the name of their son. Opi chi chi. Opi chi chi.

29 Pii gaa-ni-dgoshnawaad maa wiigwaamensing Pichi oosan
gii-madwewebdoonan mtigoon. "Ngwis," gii-kida. "Dbishkoose
wii-booni-mkadekeyin. Dbishkoose wii-bi-giiweyin."

30 Gaawii wiya gii-nkwetaagesii. Pichi ngashwan miinwaa oosan
gii-waagjiitaawag wii-biindaabwaad maa wiigwaamensing megwaa
tikwaansing. Gaa-zhi-zhichgewaad maanda, bineshiinh gii-bi-
zaagjibizad. Gaawaanh gii-mkadewaanza miinwaa gii-mkadewzid
miinwaa mskwaani kaakan. Pi chi chi pi chi chi.

31 Mii dash gii-ngamad, tikwaansing nmadbi, shpiming, maa yaayaad.

32 Mii dash gii-giigdad.

33 "Ngitziimag," kida bineshiinh, "gwaabam ezhinaagziyaanh
noongwa. Gwis gaa-aawid gii-maajaa. Zaam naa wewiib gii-zhi-
naashkowaa gojiing miinwaa zaam naa gnwenzh gii-baabiitoon
mshkoziiwin. Mii dash endsa-mnookmik ji-bi-bskaabiiyaanh pii
egzhideg gdagaaakoons nesewin bi-yaamgak maampii gdakiimnaan.
Pii noondwiwaad bemaadzijig ji-gkendmowaad mii iw pii
gwiiwzens ji-o-bwaajgeng mkadeked. Giin sa wii go kidwinan da-
naadmaagemgadoon wii-mkowaazhmadwaa o-gitziiman wii-bwaa-
njiknaawaad gwiswaan zaam gnwezh gojiing."

34 Mii dash bmi-ngamad iw ngamwin gwiswaan gaa-zhinkaaznid ow
Pichi gii-bmibza mtigwaakiing nikeyaa.

29   When they reached the lodge, Opichi's father shook the poles. "My
      son," he said, "it is time to end your fast. It is time to come home."

30   There was no answer. Opichi's mother and father bent down to look
      into the small lean-to of hemlock boughs and saplings. As they did so,
      a bird came flying out. It was gray and black with a red chest. Opi chi
      chi. Opi chi chi.

31   So it sang as it perched on a branch above them.

32   Then he spoke.

33   "My parents," said the bird, "you see me as I am now. The one who
      was your son is gone. You sent him out too early and asked him to
      wait for power too long. Now I will return each spring when the
      gentle breath of the Fawn comes to our land. My song will let people
      know it is the time for a boy to go on his dream fast. But your words
      must help to remind his parents not to make their son stay out too
      long."

34   Then, singing that song which was the name of their son, the robin
      flew off into the forest.

NOTE: Some edits were made to the Anishinaabemowin side to make the
spelling consistent with the rest of the booklet, but no new words were added.
The original published story is from Janette Richmond, "Ketsojig Aadsokaanan:
Indigenous Language from Two Elders' Perspectives," in *The Gifts Within:
Carrying Each Other forward in Aboriginal Education*, edited by Rebecca Priegert
Coulter (Ottawa: Canadian Centre for Policy Alternatives, 2009), 91–96.

Mkoons

Ira White gii-dbaajmo / Stories told by Ira White Sr.

BZHIKOOG MIINWAA BEZHIGOOGZHIIG

1 Ira ndizhinikaaz. Mkoons ge nishinaabemkaazayaanh.

2 Ira White Sr. Mii dash *My mother was* Ferrin Riley.

3 *Ferrin* was a name that was hardly known or used. But after she passed away, there was my great-nieces; they were named after her.

4 Ngitziimag pane gii-nishnaabemwag.

5 Mii dash gwiiwzenswiyaanh go naa gii-ni-gkendmaanh ezhi-kidwaad gegoo.

6 Mii go genii gaa-zhi-kidayaanh ekdowaad.

7 Giishpin bzhikoog gii-dbaajmowaad mii go genii gii-dbaajmoyaanh genii wii-zhi-nishnaabe ngii-waabmaag ko.

8 Mii dash ngii-wiindmowaa gaa-waabmagwaa genii chi-bzhikoog miinwaa bezhigogzhiig bmiptoowag ko pipiichin.

9 Gii-bbaambatoowag go naa. Kina go naa mnisheying maampii. *Highbanks, Backsettlement,* nooj go naa gii-bbaa-yaawag. Nookming ge go. Biinji-nookming. Gii-bbaa-shaangshinwaad oodi.

10 Wenda go naa gii-miikanaakewag ge go oodi nookming bmosewaad pane maa aazhook bmosewaad mii go maapiich miikaans gii-bmi-yaamgak maa ezhi-bmosewaad bzhikoog miinwaa bezhgoogzhiig.

COWS AND HORSES

1 My name is Ira, and I'm called Mkoons in Anishinaabemowin.

2 Ira White Sr. Then my mother was Ferrin Riley.

3 Ferrin was a name that was hardly known or used. But after she passed away, there was my great-nieces; they were named after her.

4 My parents always spoke Anishinaabemowin

5 Then, when I was a boy, I started to understand what they were saying.

6 That's how I said what they said.

7 If they told stories about cows, I would tell stories in the language too, that I use to see them.

8 Then I told them how I use to see big cows and horses running around from time to time.

9 They ran around all over the island here. Highbanks, Backsettlement, they were all over the place. At the bush too. In the bush, they laid around over there.

10 They made a lot of trails over there in the bush when they were always walking around there, walking back and forth on the trails, and they'd eventually start to make a pathway here when the cows and horses walked.

WENDA GO GII-BOOZMOWAG

1 Weweni go. Wena go. Wenda go. Gii-boozmowag go naa.

2 Kina gegoo go naa gii-dbaajmowaad engoonh, zhashkoonyag, mzhweyag, san'gooyag, kina go naa.

3 Pane go naa gii-nishnaabemtoogwaa. Miinwaa go waa-zhichgeyaang owedi nookming wiin sa gwa.

4 Jidmoonyag miinwaa waabshkokiing oodi zhashkoonyag. Mii sa iw.

THEY SPOKE VERY FLUENTLY

1   Very well. Really well. They spoke very fluently.

2   They talked about everything, ants, muskrats, rabbits, chipmunks. Everything.

3   I would always be talking them as we were working in the bush.

4   Squirrels and muskrats in the marsh. That's it.

BEZHGOOGZHIIG

1 Bezhgogzhiig ge go gii-yaawag ko maampii mnisheyiing. Nooj go
naa gii-naanzawag.

2 Mkadewnaagziwag pipiichin giishpin go naa bzhikoog ge go ngii-
waabmaag. Gii-bbaambatoowag miikanaang wedi.

3 Chi-mbull go naa ngii-waabmaa wodi biidaasmosed. Wenda go
gii-nshkaadzi. Mii go naa gii-gjibweyaanh wii-bwaa-....Mii gaa-zhi-d
...wedi chi-mbull.

4 Mii sa iw egkendmaanh. Aaniish go naa gii-yaawag oodi
bezhgoogzhiig miinwaa bzhikoog.

5 Mewnzha go naa gii-yaawag. Wodi nikaang iw nookming miinwaa
miikanaang miinwaa waabshkokiing ngii-waabmaag ko.

6 Bmosewaad oodi. Chi-mbull go naa miinwaa bzhikoog. Niibna go
naa. Mii sa iw.

HORSES

1 Horses use to be here on the island too. They were different colors.

2 They looked black from time to time, if [I saw them], and I saw cows too. They ran around on the road over there.

3 I saw a big bull as he was walking toward me. He was really angry. So I ran away ... That's ... the big bull over there.

4 That's what I knew. Well, the horses and cows were over there.

5 A long time ago they were there. I use to see them in the bush and on the road and in the marsh.

6 When they walked over there, the big bull and the cows, there were lots of them. That's it.

CHI-GNEBIGOOG

1 Ngii-waabmaag ko gnebigoog oodi bmoodewaad. Chi-gnebigoog oodi waabshkokiing.

2 Miinwaa enji … dkonweniniwag oodi nokiiwaad miikanong. Ngii-waabmaag chi-gnebigoog oodi bmoodewaad wodi wenda go ngii-zegigoog ko ge gii-waabmagwaa.

3 Niibna dshing go ngii-waabmaan oodi bmikwed oodi naa miikanaang.

4 Mii dash ngii-wiindmowaag ngitziimag gaa-zhi-waabmagwaa.

5 Bezhig chi-gnebig gchinaatig oodi bmaangza gaa-zhinaagzid oodi gii-waabmag.

6 Wenda go ngii-zegiz, gii-nnangbizayaanh go naa gii-waabmag epiichi-mididad iw chi-gnebig. Chi-gnebigoog.

7 Wenda go gaa wiikaa ngii-waabmaasii baamaa go naa gii-baamseyaanh wodi miinwaa daabaan … daabaangoyaanh wodi gii-waabmagwaa wodi.

8 Mii sa iw.

BIG SNAKES

1   I use to see snakes crawling over there, big snakes over there in the marsh.

2   And where ... the police station is over there on that road, I saw big snakes over there crawling, and they use to scare me when I saw them.

3   A lot of times I saw the tracks over there on the road.

4   Then I told my parents I saw them.

5   One big snake lying on the road that looked like a big stick when I saw him.

6   I was so scared that I was trembling over there when I saw how big that snake was. The snakes.

7   I never really saw one until I was walking around over there, and as I was driving ... driving around, that's when I saw them over there.

8   That's it.

NGII-BBAA-NIIGE GO

1   Ngii-bbaa-niige go genii.

2   Ge gsha gwiiwzenswiyaanh zhashkoonyag ngii-bbaa-ndowaabmaag
miinwaa esbaanyag ngii-bbaa-ndowaabmaag. Wiin sa gwa. Mii
dash wii-daaweyaanh, iw sa *how do you say that 'fur'?* {Biiway} aanii?
{Biiway} enh, mii iw. Gii-bbaa-daaweyaanh genii gii-shkwaa-nsagwaa
zhashkoonyag miinwaa esbaanyag.

3   Naangodnong jidmoonyag ge go ngii-nsaag ge go wii-miijyaang iw
sa zhashkoonh miinwaa jidmoonh wiiyaas. Mii sa iw.

4   Mnapgoziwag go. Gechwaa naa gaakwaanh.

5   Ndigitziimag gii-bkon'gewaad miinwaa gii-... *how do you say he
put him in a frying pan and cook him? ...* gii-zaasgokwaanaa? ... Enh,
gii-zaasgokwaanaad, *my mother.* San'goonyag, mzhiwenh, pipiichin
zhashkoonyag ge go. Kina sko naa gii-mnapgoziwag.

6   Ngii-ndamoojge ge go pipiichin.

7   Ngii-zhitoon go naa waa-naabwagwaa maampii dooning.

8   Ngii-waabmaag go naa emkozhwewaad pagdoweyaanh wedi
miinwaa biinji-... *how do you say "winding in"?*

9   *Yeah.* Ngii-waabmaa go naa nooj go ... *they were biting that bait. It got
hooked on their mouths.*

I WENT AROUND TRAPPING

1   I went trapping too.

2   And when I was a little boy, I'd go looking around for muskrats and racoons to kill, those ones. Then I'd go sell them, that, how do you say that "fur"? {Biiway.} What? {Biiway.} Yeah that's it. I went around selling them too after killing muskrats and racoons.

3   Sometimes I killed squirrels too, and also to eat muskrat and squirrel meat. That's it.

4   They tasted good, just like chicken.

5   My parents skinned him and ... how do you say he put him in a frying pan and cook him? ... gii-zaasgokwaanaa? ... Yeah, she fried him, my mother. Chipmunks, rabbits, sometimes muskrats too. All of them tasted good.

6   I went fishing, too, from time to time.

7   I use to make a hook to hook them here in the mouth.

8   I saw them swim when I threw it in over there in ... how do you say "winding in"?

9   I saw her doing various ... they were biting that bait. It got hooked on their mouths.

10   So I'm gonna maampii doopwining ngii-saa. *I put him there on the table.*

11   Mii dash ngii- ... gii ... *what do you call when you scale them?*

12   *I haven't said that word in a long time. That's the way it is I guess when I don't speak it too often.*

13   *But when my folks were living,* pane go naa gii-nishnaabemtoogwaa.

10   So I'm gonna put it here on the table. I put him there on the table.

11   Then I ... [past tense marker] ... what do you call when you scale them?

12   I haven't said that word in a long time. That's the way it is I guess when I don't speak it too often.

13   But when my folks were living, I always spoke Anishinaabemowin to them.

GII-NOKIIYAANH CHI-MOOKMAANKIING

1 Ngii-nokii go naa ngoding oodi nikeyaa.

2 Gii-shkinwewseyaanh. Gii-shkinwewyaanh go naa.

3 Ngii-nokii oodi.

4 Ngii-zhitoonan go naa *what ya call 'em? Clay plates. Plates and bowls and dishes and the pottery.*

5 Enh, oodi nikeyaa. Mt. *Clemens.* Enh, ngii-nokii oodi. Wenjda go naa ngii-nokii oodi.

6 Enh, gnwezh go.

7 Ngii-wiijnokiimaag ko zhaagnaashag, miinwaa Mexicans, Nishnaabeg gye go.

8 Zhaagnaashag ge go. nooj go naa. Mkade…aanii waa-kidayaanh?… mkadeninwag ge go gii-nokiiwag oodi. *Four nationalities. Four or five.*

9 Aanind go naa ngii-gnoonaag. Zaam go naa gii-…gnwezh go…I *didn't know them very well.*

10 *I didn't say too much to them. One time, I seen a Mexican. I thought he was a nishnaab. I said, "Aaniish naa ezhi-bmaadziyin?" He said, "Oh, I don't speak that."*

11 Mii go naa gaa-nenmag Anishinaabe aawid.

WHEN I WORKED IN THE UNITED STATES

1   I worked over that way.

2   When I was a young man. A young man.

3   I worked over there.

4   I made, what ya call 'em? Clay plates. Plates and bowls and dishes and the pottery.

5   Yeah, over that way, Mt. Clemens. Yeah, I worked over there. I worked there for a long time.

6   Yeah, for a long time.

7   I use to work with white people, Mexicans, and Anishinaabe people too.

8   White people, various [kinds of people], black ... How do I say? ... black people worked over there too. Four nationalities. Four or five.

9   I talked to some of them. Because ... for a long time ... I didn't know them very well.

10   I didn't say too much to them. One time, I seen a Mexican. I thought he was a nishnaab. I said, "How are you living?" He said, "Oh, I don't speak that."

11   I thought he was an Anishinaabe.

12 {Aaniish gaa-zhinkaadameg 'Mexicans'?}

13 Gaawii gnabaj ndo-gkendziin iw. Gegaa shwii go Anishinaabe
    ezhinaagziwaad oodi nikeyaa.

12   {What do you all call "Mexicans"?}

13   I don't really know that. But they almost look like Anishinaabe people over there.

MAATOOKII ENWEYING

1   Mii go iw nikeyaa. Maapiich giinaa gegaa go naa ngii-wnitoon nishnaabemyaanh.

2   Zaam go naa zhaagnaashii-gnoonaag pane. Mii-sh go eta zhaagnaashiimyaanh oodi Waabganoojiinaang. *Wallaceburg was known as* Waabganoojiinaang. *Use to be a lot of rats and mice over there in Wallaceburg. So they call it* 'Waabganoojiinaang.'

3   Gaa-ndaawaad oodi iidig.

4   Oh chi-nendaagod gnabaj iw.

5   Chi-nendaagod. Daa-gyako binoojiinyag gkinoomaagoowaad getzijig wii-gkendmowaad go gwiiwzensag miinwaa kwezensag waa-ni-nikeyaa waa-ni-nishnaabemwaad.

6   Mii go naa gaashiiwag mii go gkendmowaad pane nishinaabemtowaad ngoji, miikanaang, kina go naa mnisheying.

7   Miikanaang oodi bmosewaad. Mii go naa giishpin go naa wiindmowaad "Aapiish ezhaayin?" "Oh wedi nikeyaa nii-zhaa."

8   Maapiich go naa Ga-ni-gkendmowaad waa-zhi-nikeyaa, waa-kidawaad gegoo.

9   *They'll know how to say after a while when they teach them many times.*

SHARING OUR LANGUAGE

1   That's the way. Eventually I almost lost how to speak
    Anishinaabemowin.

2   Because I always speak English to everyone. I only speak
    English over there in Wallaceburg. Wallaceburg was known as
    Waabganoojiinaang. Use to be a lot of rats and mice over there in
    Wallaceburg. So they call it Waabganoojiinaang.

3   They must live over there.

4   I think it's really important.

5   It is really worth something. It would be good for the children to
    be taught from the elders, so the boys and girls know how to speak
    Anishinaabemowin in that way.

6   When they're small they know how to speak Anishinaabemowin
    anywhere, on the road, everywhere on the island.

7   When they're walking over there on the road. If they tell them
    "Where you going?" "Oh I'm going over there."

8   Eventually, they'll know how to say it that way, how to say anything.

9   They'll know how to say after a while when they teach them many
    times.

10   {Niin, mbegish naa nishinaabemwaad binoojiinyag. Nbgosendam.}

11   Mii go genii naasaab. Wii-bwaa-wnitoowaad nishnaabemwin.

12   Pane go naa daa-nishinaabemtowaad gwiiwzensag miinwaa
     kwezensag wii-bwaa-wnitoowaad iw sa nishnaabemwin.

13   Mii sa iw.

10   {I hope the children speak Anishinaabemowin.}

11   I think the same, for them to not lose Anishinaabemowin.

12   They should always speak to the boys and girls so they don't lose
       Anishinaabemowin.

13   That's it.

Kaangaadese

Edwin Taylor gii-dbaajma / Republished story told by Edwin Taylor

GAA-ZHI-DGOSHNOOMGAK MSHKIKIIN

1 Niibna dbik gii-zoogpii:

2 Aanind bineshiinyag gii-maawnjidiwag, gaawii go kina, aanind enshkaadzijig bineshiinyag gii-maawnjidiwag, mii dash gii-gnoondiwaad.

3 Gii-nshkaadziitwaawaan Anishinaaben, mii maa naa gii-giiwsaangowaad.

4 "The Anishinaabeg ngiiwsaanigonaanig miinwạa baashkzigonaanig wii-debnamwaad miijim."

5 Gii-nshkaaji-gaagiigdowag. "Meshtooj gegoo gdaa-doodwaanaanig." "Wenesh waa-zhichgeying?", gii-kwejdiwag.

6 "Aaa, aakziwin ga-biidmowaanaanig giw Anishinaabeg. Nga-ndamaanaanig giw aanind bineshiinyag (migiziwag, gekekoog, gookookoog …) miinwaa ga-kwejmaanaanig wii-bi-nmadbiwaad gewii giigdaying.

7 Mii dash, gii-ndamaawaad niw aanind bineshiinyan mii sa go gii-maawnji-giigdowaad.

8 Giw aanind bineshiinyag gii-noondaagewag giw mji-bineshiinyag gaa-kidwaad, waa-zhi-aakzii'aawaad Anishinaaben. Gii-shkwaa-bzindwaawaad niw enshkaadzinjin, giw aanind bineshiinyag kidwag, "Kaa gaawiin."

HOW THE MEDICINES CAME INTO BEING

1   Niibna dbik gii-zoogpii (many moons ago):

2   Some birds got together, not all the birds, but some angry birds got together, and held council.

3   They were angry at the Anishinaabeg for hunting them for food.

4   "The Anishinaabeg hunt us and shoot us for food."

5   They spoke angrily amongst themselves. "Let us get them back." "What can we do, to get the Anishinaabeg?" they asked each other.

6   "Ahh, we will bring disease and sickness to the Anishinaabeg. We will call on the other birds, (eagles, hawks, owls ...) and ask them to join us in council."

7   And so, they called on the other birds and they held council together.

8   The other birds listened to the plan of the angry birds, of how they wanted to bring disease and sickness to the Anishinaabeg. After listening to the angry birds, all the other birds said, "Kaa gaawiin."

9   "Gaa maamdaa wii-naadmaageyaang wii-debnadwaa giw
     Anishinaabeg. Pii giiwsewaad Anishinaabeg, gchi-piitenmaawaan
     Gzhe-mnidoon. Giishpin geniinwi zhichgeyaang waa-zhichgeyeg,
     gaawii weweni nda-wiijiiwaasii Gzhe-mnidoo. Gaawii maamdaa
     wii-naadmaagooyeg."

10   Mii dash kina gii-ni-maamaajaawaad.

11   Giw bineshiinyag gaa-nshkaadzijig, nwanj gii-nshkaadziwag.
     "Wenesh waa-zhichgeying, wii-debnangwaa giw Anishinaabeg?"

12   "Giw aanind bineshiinyag wii-naadmaagesiiwag." Gii-nshkaaji-
     gnoondiwag.

13   "Aaa, gdaa-ndamaanaanig wesiinyag miinwaa ga-kwejmaanaanig
     wii-waawye-nmadbiwaad. Ga-naadmaagonaanig. Anishinaabeg
     giiwsaanaawaan miinwaa bashkzwaawaan gewii."

14   Mii dash, gii-ndamaawaan wesiinyan mii dash gii-maawnji-
     giigdowaad.

15   Wesiinyag gii-noondwaawaan niw enshkaadzinjin bineshiinyan,
     waa-zhi-aakzii'aawaad Anishinaaben.

16   Gii-shkwaa-bzindwaawaad niw enshkaadzinjin bineshiinyan, kina
     wesiinyag kidwag, "Kaa gaawiin."

17   "Gaa maamdaa wii-naadmaageyaang wii-debnadwaa giw
     Anishinaabeg. Pii giiwsewaad Anishinaabeg, gchi-piitendaagewag.
     Giishpin geniinwi zhichgeyaang waa-zhichgeyeg, gaawii
     weweni nda-wiijiiwaasii Gzhe-mnidoo. Gaawii maamdaa wii-
     naadmaagooyeg."

18   Mii dash kina gii-ni-maamaajaawaad.

9   "We cannot join you in your plan to get the Anishinaabeg. For when the Anishinaabeg hunt for food, they do it in a respectful way. And for us to join you in your evil plan would be to go against the way of the Creator. We will not join you."

10   And so, they broke up council.

11   The angry birds were now even angrier. "What can we do to get the Anishinaabeg?"

12   "The other birds will not join us." They spoke angrily amongst themselves.

13   "Ah, we will call on the animals and ask them to join us in council. They will help us. The Anishinaabeg hunt and shoot them for food also."

14   And so they called on the animals, and they held council together.

15   The animals listened to the plan of the angry birds, of how they wanted to bring disease and sickness to the Anishinaabeg.

16   After listening to the angry birds, all the animals said, "Kaa gaawiin."

17   "We cannot join you in your plan to get the Anishinaabeg. For when the Anishinaabeg hunt for food, they do it in a respectful way. And for us to join you in your evil plan would be to go against the way of the Creator. We will not join you."

18   And so they broke up council.

19   Giw bineshiinyag gaa-nshkaadzijig, nwanj gii-nshkaadziwag.
     "Wenesh waa-zhichgeying wii-debnangwaa giw Anishinaabeg?"

20   "Wesiinyag wii-naadmaagesiiwag ge wiinwaa." Gii-mji-gaagiidowag
     gnoondiwaad.

21   "Aaa, ga-kwejmaanaanig giw ezaagkiijig wii-bi-waawye-
     nmadbiwaad. Ga-naadmaagonaanig."

22   Mii dash gii-ndamaawaad ezaagkiinjin mii dash gii-waawye-
     dbiwaad.

23   Egtigaadegin gii-noondaagewag giw mji-bineshiinyag gaa-kidwaad,
     waa-zhi-aakzii'aawaad Anishinaaben.

24   Gii-shkwaa-bzindwaawaad niw enshkaadzinjin, giw aanind
     ezaagkiijig ekidwaad, "Kaa gaawiin."

25   "Gaa maamdaa wii-naadmaageyaang wii-debnadwaa giw
     Anishinaabeg. Pii giiwsewaad Anishinaabeg, gchi-piitendaagewag.
     Gaawii maamdaa wii-naadmaagooyeg."

26   Mii dash kina gii-ni-maamaajaawaad.

27   Giw bineshiinyag gaa-nshkaadzijig, nwanj gii-nshkaadziwag.

28   Egtigaadegin gii-nendmoog wii-waawye-dbiwaad, wiinwaa gwa.

29   Gii-gchi-dnenmaawaan niw Anishinaaben, miinwaa giw
     enshkaadzijig bneshiinyag waa-zhichgewaad.

30   "Wenesh waa-zhichgeying wii-naadmangidwaa giw Anishinaabeg?"
     gii-kwejdiwag.

19   The angry birds were now even angrier. "What can we do to get the Anishinaabeg?"

20   "The animals will not join us either." They spoke angrily amongst themselves.

21   "Ah, we will call on the plants and ask them to join us in council. They will help us."

22   And so, they called on the plants, and they held council together.

23   The plants listened to the plan of the angry birds, of how they wanted to bring disease and sickness to the Anishinaabeg.

24   After listening to the angry birds, all the plants said, "Kaa gaawiin."

25   "We cannot join you in your plan to get the Anishinaabeg. For when the Anishinaabeg hunt for food, they do it in a respectful way. And for us to join you in your evil plan would be go against the way of the Creator. We will not join you."

26   And so they broke up council.

27   The angry birds were now even angrier.

28   The plants decided to hold council together again, amongst themselves.

29   They were very concerned for the Anishinaabeg and the angry birds' evil plan.

30   "What can we do to help the Anishinaabeg?" they asked each other.

31 "Aabdeg ga-naadmowaanaanig Anishinaabeg. Giw enshkaadzijig
bineshiinyag gegoo wii-zhichgewag. Wenesh waa-zhichgeying?"
Gii-kwedwewag egtigaadegin gewiinwaa.

32 "Aaa, ga-miindizmi wii-noojmowaad miinwaa wii-mno-yaawaad giw
Anishinaabeg. Ga-zhinkaandizmi, 'mshkiki'. Kina maawnji-yaaying
mshkikiin ga-zhinkaazmi."

33 Mii dash iw mshkikiin gaa-zhi-debnamaang.

34 Mshkikiin geyaabi nakiimigadoon, naadmowaawaad Anishinaaben
wii-bwaa-aakzinid.

35 Miinwaa giw enshkaadzijig bineshiinyag geyaabi kweji-mji-
doodaagewag.

31   "We must help the Anishinaabeg. Those angry birds are going to try
      to carry out their plan. What can we do?" asked the plants amongst
      themselves.

32   "Ah, we will offer ourselves up to the Anishinaabeg for healing and
      wellness. We shall call ourselves mshkiki. All of us together shall be
      called mshkikiin."

33   And that is how the medicines came into being.

34   The mshkikiin are still doing their job today, helping the
      Anishinaabeg to fight against disease and sickness.

35   And the angry birds are still trying to carry out their evil plan
      [e.g., avian flu].

NOTE: Some edits were made to the Anishinaabemowin side to make the
spelling consistent with the rest of the booklet, but no new words were
added. The original published story is from Janette Richmond, "Ketsojig
Aadsokaanan: Indigenous Language from Two Elders' Perspectives," in The
Gifts Within: Carrying Each Other forward in Aboriginal Education, edited by Rebecca
Priegert Coulter (Ottawa: Canadian Centre for Policy Alternatives, 2009),
98–102.

Glossary

The following is a list of the words from the stories in this book, since not every line has a word for word translation. Italics have been used in some of the words to indicate less common pronunciations. Also, each word is listed in its most basic form as possible. If you would like to learn more about the grammar structure of Anishinaabemowin, you can seek out the following publications:

· Rand Valentine, *Nishnaabemwin Reference Grammar* (Toronto: University of Toronto Press, 2001)
· Brendan Fairbanks, *Ojibwe Discourse Markers* (Lincoln: University of Nebraska Press, 2016)
· Michael D. Sullivan Sr., *Relativization in Ojibwe* (Lincoln: University of Nebraska Press, 2020)
· Mary Ann Corbiere, *Nishnaabemwin Workbooks & Lexicon* (Sudbury, Ontario: University of Sudbury, Department of Native Studies, 2007)

KEY TO GLOSSARY

Adverb = av

Conjunction = cj

Interjection = ij

Noun animate = na

Noun inanimate = ni

Number = nm

Particle/discourse marker = pt

Prenoun = pn

Preverb = pv

Proper noun animate = pr-an

Proper noun inanimate = pr-in

Quantity = qnt

Verb animate intransitive = vai

Verb animate intransitive plural = vaip

Verb intransitive inanimate = vii

Verb transitive animate = vta

Verb transitive inanimate = vti

KIDWINAN—WORDS

Aabdeg (av): Have to/certainly

Aabji'aa (vta): S/he is using it (animate)

Aabjitoon (vti): S/he is using it

Aabnaabi (vai): S/he is looking back

Aaboodaasin (vii): It flips over in the wind

Aadaakwaan (vti): S/he is locking it

Aadshin (vai): S/he is marooned/ stranded

Aakziwin (ni): Sickness

Aana (av): In vain/to no avail

Aaniinde (av): Of course/naturally

Aaniish (av): What?/How?/Why?

Aaniish go naa (pt): "What the heck?" (expression)

Aanind (av): Some/a few

Aankanootwaa (vta): S/he is translating him/her

Aanziiyaan(an) (ni): Diaper(s)

Aapiish (av): Where? (in a question)

Aapji (av): Very/completely

Aawi (vai): S/he is certain person/thing

Aazhbikoons (ni): Hill

Aazhook (av): Back and forth

Aazhwaakwaa (av): "Backsettlement" on Bkejwanong/Other side of the woods

Ahaaw (ij): OK

Amik (na): Beaver

Anishinaabe (na): Ojibwe/Anishinaabe person

Anishinaabemo (vai): S/he speaks Ojibwe

Anishinaabemowin (ni): Anishinaabe language

Anishinaabemwin (*alternate spelling*) (ni): Anishinaabe language

Anishinaabewinikaaza (vai): His/her Anishinaabe name

Baabiichge (vai): S/he is waiting

Baabiitoon (vti): S/he is waiting for it

Baagaakogan(ag) (na): Splint(s) (basket making)

Baagaakoge (vai): S/he is pounding wood (basket)

Baapi (vai): S/he is laughing

Baashkzwaa (vta): S/he is shooting him/her

Baatiinad (vii): To be a lot/be plentiful (inanimate)

Baatiinwag (vaip): To be a lot/be plentiful (animate)

Bbaa-/paa- (pv): Moving about/going around

Bbaambatoo (vai): S/he is running around

Bbaanjiiwyaawni (vai): S/he is hanging around

Bbaanjiptoo (vai): S/he running around

Bbaa-yaa (vai): S/he is going around

Bboongizi (vai): S/he is so many years

Bejiiwii (vai): S/he is physically weak

Bemaadzijig (na): People

Besho/Besha (av): Close/near

Bezhgoogzhii (na): Horse

Bezhgonong (av): In the same way/
manner

Bezhig (nm): One

Bgidendiwag (vaip): They let go of one
another

Bgidenmaa (vta): S/he is burying him/
her

Bgosendam (vai): S/he hopes/wishes

Bi- (pv): (An action) in this direction

Bi (vai): It (animate) is at a certain place

Bi-giiwe (vai): S/he is coming home

Biibaagi (vai): S/he is shouting/
whooping

Biibaagmaa (vta): S/he is calling/
shouting out to him/her

Biibiins (na): Baby

Biidaaban (vii): It is dawn/light in the
early morning

Biidaasmose (vai): S/he is walking this
way

Biidmowaa (vta): S/he is bring it for
him/her

Biidoon (vti): S/he is bringing it

Biidwewebtoo (vai): S/he is coming
running this way

Biidweweshin (vai): S/he is heard
(steps) approaching

Biigbidoon (vti): S/he is breaking it
(with hands)

Biinaa (vta): S/he brings s/he/it
animate

Biinaabminaagod (vii): It is clean/It
looks clean

Biinaagmi (vii): It is clean (water/
liquid)

Biinaagmisin (vii): It is clean (body of
water)

Biinaagod (vii): It is clean

Biindge (vai): S/he is entering

Biindig (av): Inside

Biingeji (vai): S/he is cold

Biiskaan (vti): S/he is wearing it

Biiskowaa (vta): S/he is wearing it
(animate)

Biiszhwaa (vta): S/he is cutting it
(animate) into pieces

Biiway (ni): Fur/wool/yarn

Biiweziimag (na): Family

Bineshiinh(yag) (na): Bird(s)

Bi-njibaa (vai): S/he comes from a
certain place

Bi-njiwse (vai): S/he is coming walking

Binoojiinh (na): Child

Binoojiinswi (vai): S/he is a small child

Binoojiinwi (vai): S/he is a child

Bi-yaa (vai): S/he is coming (in this
direction)

Bkaan (vii): It is different

Bkejwanong (ni): Formerly Walpole
Island, Ontario

Bkinaage (vai): S/he is winning

Bkong'e (vai): S/he is skinning
(animals)

Bmaadzi (vai): S/he is living/is alive

Bmaangza (vai): S/he is lying around

Bmi- (pv): Go by (doing something/
time)

Bmibde (vii): It is flying along/by

Bmibza (vai): S/he is flying along/by

Bmikwe (vai): S/he leaves footprints/
tracks

Bmiptoo (vai): S/he is running along

Bmiwdoon (vti): S/he is carrying it

Bmizaakii (vai): S/he is going out (of a place)

Bmizaakmo (vai): S/he is going out

Bmoode (vai): S/he is crawling

Bmose (vai): S/he is walking

Bnaajchige (vai): S/he is ruining things

Bngishin (vai): S/he is falling down/ tripping fall

Boodaajge (vai): S/he is blowing air

Boodaajgemigad (vii): It is blowing air

Booni- (pv): Stop doing/being something

Booniikwaa (vta): S/he is leaving him/ her alone

Boontaa (vai): S/he is stopping/quitting

Boozhoo (ij): Hello

Boozmo (vai): S/he is speaking fluently

Booztoon (vti): S/he is loading something into a vehicle

Bskaabii (vai): S/he is returning

Bskaabiimigad (vii): It is returning

Bwaa- (pv): Not/so that not

Bwaajige (vai): S/he is dreaming

Bwaajigewin (ni): Dream

Bzhik(oog) (na): Cow(s)

Bzindaajgaaza (vai): S/he is listened to

Bzindaan (vti): S/he is listening to it

Bzindwaa (vta): S/he is listening to him/her

Chigaade (vii): It is being put/placed somewhere

Chi-gamiing (av): Across the lake/ ocean

Chi-mookmaankiing (ni): United States/Big Knife Land

Chi-nendaagod (vii): It is important/ highly thought of

Daa (vai): S/he lives at a certain place

Daa- (pv): Could/can/would/should

Daabaan(ag) (na): Car(s)

Daabaango (vai): S/he is driving

Daan (vti): S/he is talking about/means something

Daangnaa (vta): S/he is touching him/ her

Daapnaa (vta): S/he is picking him/her/ it (animate) up

Daawe (vai): S/he is selling things

Daawegamig (ni): Store

Damiiyaawshkaagon (vai): It's his responsibility/job

Damna (vai): S/he is playing

Dash (av): Then/though/and so

Dawemaan (na): His/her relative

Dbaajdaan (vti): S/he is talking about it

Dbaajdiza (vai): S/he is telling a story about oneself

Dbaajmaa (vta): S/he is talking about him/her

Dbaajmo (vai): S/he is telling a story

Dbaajmotaadiwag (vaip): They are telling each other stories

Dbaajmotowaa (vta): S/he is telling a story to him/her

Dbendawaa (vta): S/he is staying over at his/her house

Dbi (av): Wherever/don't know where

Dbishkoose (vii): Come around/mark a certain time

Dchiwag (vaip): To be such a number

Debaabmaa (vta): S/he sees him/her from a distance

Debenjiged (na): Creator/one who owns things

Debnaa (vta): S/he got him/her/reached him/her

Debnaak (av): As long as/provided that

Debnaak (av): Carelessly

Debnaan (vti): S/he reached and grabbed it/caught it

Debse (vii): It is enough/It suffices

Debwe'aandam (vai): S/he believe it

Debwetwaa (vta): S/he believes him/her

Detewaakoge (vai): S/he is knocking (on a door)

Dewegan(ag) (na): Drum(s)

Dewege/Dewe'ige (vai): S/he is drumming

Dgoshin (vai): S/he is arriving

Dibikad/Dbikad (vii): It is dark

Dibikong (av): Last night

Dibziibi (av): Edge of the river

Dinmaagan(an) (na): Shoulder(s)

Dkeyaa (vii): It is cool (weather)

Dkonaan (vti): Holding something (off the floor)

Dnakmigzi (vai): S/he is busying oneself

Dnenmaa (vta): S/he is concerned for/expect someone

Dnowan (pr-in): Kind/sort

Doodaage (vai): S/he is doing (something)

Doodwaa (vta): S/he is doing something to him/her

Doopwin(an) (ni): Table(s)

Dsa- (pv): So many of/number of/every

Dshing (av): A certain number of times

Dzhi- (pv): At a certain place/where

Dzhimaa (vta): S/he is talking about him/her

Dzhindaan (vti): S/he is talking about it

Egtigaadegin (ni): Plants

Endaad (ni): His/her house

Endaayaanh (ni): My home/where I dwell

Endgwenh (av): I wonder/I don't know whether or not

En'goonh (na): Ant

Enh (ij): Yes/in agreement

Esbaanh (na): Raccoon

Eshkam (av): Increasingly/more and more

Esnaa (av): Ever (used emphatically)

Eta (av): Only/just

Ewaabshkiiwed (na): White being

Ezaagkiijig (na): Plants (animate)

Gaa- (pv): Changed form past tense

Gaachii (vai): S/he is small

Gaachninjii (vai): S/he has small hands

Gaa-giiwsejig (na): Hunters

Gaakwaanh (na): Chicken

Gaa maamdaa (pt): Can't

Gaaming (av): Across a body of water

Gaashii (vai): S/he is small

Gaashiiwi (vai): S/he is small

Gaashin(oon) (vii): It is small/they are small

Gaaskzidebooza (vai): His/her feet making shuffling sounds

Gaawaanh (av): Barely/hardly

Gaawiin (av): No/not

Gaazhgenh (na): Cat

Ganamaa (av): Maybe/perhaps

Gashwan (na): His/her mother

Gbe'iing (av): For a long time

Gchi-/Chi- (pn): Big/great/major

Gchi-/Chi- (pv): Much/extremely/ very/hard

Gchi-gaaming (av): Overseas

Gchinaatig (na): Big stick

Gchi-nendam (vai): S/he is happy/ proud

Gchi-piitendaage (vai): S/he does things in a respectful way

Gchi-piitendaagod (vii): It is sacred/ respected

Gchi-piitendaagzi (vai): S/he is highly respected/valued

Gchi-piitendam (vai): S/he thinks highly of it

Gchi-piitenmaa (vta): S/he respects/ thinks highly of him/her

Gdagaakoons (na): Fawn

Ge (av): And/also

Ge- (pv): Will/can (changed conjunct)

Gechwaa (av): Like/Just like

Gegek (na): Hawk

Geget (av): Really/of course/truly

Gegiin (pr-an): You too

Gegnaa (ge go naa) (pt): Emphatic marker

Gegoo (pr-in): Something

Gekaanh/Gekaanyag (na): Elder/elders

Geniin (pr-an): Me too

Geniinwi (pr-an): Us (exclusive) too

Gesganaa (av): Suddenly/immediately

Gesnaa (av): Ever/excessively/ extremely

Gete'ii (ni): Old thing

Gewe (pt): Also/as well

Gewii/Ge'ii (pr-an): Him/her too

Gewiinwaa (pr-an): Them too

Geyaabi (av): Still/more

Gii- (pv): Past tense

Giibshe (vai): S/he is deaf

Giigido/Giigida (vai): S/he is talking

Giigoonke (vai): S/he is fishing

Giikaandiwag (vaip): They are arguing

Giikmaa (vta): S/he is preaching to/ advising him/her

Giin (pr-an): You

Giinwaa (pr-an): You all

Giisaadendam (vai): S/he is regretful/ feels sorry

Giisaadkamik (ij): It's unfortunate/ It's sad

Giishenh (ni): A little bit

Giishin (cj): If

Giishkboojge (vai): S/he is sawing/ crosscutting

Giishkshwaa (vta): S/he is cutting it (animate)

Giishnadmowaa (vta): S/he is buying it for him/her

Giishnadoon (vti): S/he is buying it

Giishpin (cj): If

Giiwe (vai): S/he is going home

Giiwednong (av): In the north/to the north

Giiwenh (av): Apparently/supposedly

Giiwewdoon (vti): S/he is taking/bringing it home

Giiwewnaa (vta): S/he is taking him/her home

Giiwsaanaa (vta): S/he hunting him/her

Giiwse (vai): S/he is hunting

Giiyakwaabi (vai): S/he has good vision

Giizhgad (vii): It is day

Giizhiitaa (vai): S/he is finished (doing something)

Giizis (na): Moon/sun

Gindaan (vti): S/he is reading/counting it

Gindaasa (vai): S/he is reading/counting

Gitziiman (na): His/her parents

Giw (pr-an): Those (animate)

Gjib'aa (vta): S/he escapes from someone

Gjibwe (vai): S/he is running away

Gkendaagzi (vai): S/he is evident/known

Gkendaan (vti): S/he knows it

Gkenmaa (vta): S/he knows him/her/it (animate)

Gkinoomaage (vai): S/he is teaching

Gkinoomaagewgamig (ni): School

Gkinoomaagzi (vai): S/he is learning

Gkinoomowaa (vta): S/he is teaching him/her

Gmiwan (vii): It is raining

Gnaajwan (vii): It is beautiful

Gnabaj (av): Maybe/perhaps/probably

Gnawaabmaa (vta): S/he is looking at him/her

Gnawenmaa (vta): S/he is looking after him/her

Gnebig(oog) (na): Snake(s)

Gnige (av): Even/at least

Gnoonaa (vta): S/he is talking to him/her

Gnoondiwag (vaip): They are talking to each other

Gnooyaa(noon) (vii): It is long/They are long

Gnwezh (av): Long time

Go/Gwa (pt): Indeed

Gojiing (av): Outside/outdoors

Gokbinaagaans(an) (ni): Little basket(s)

Gokbinaagan(an) (ni): Basket(s)

Gokbinaaganike (vai): S/he is making baskets

Gonaajwan/Gnaajwan (vii): It is beautiful

Gonda (pr-an): These (animate)

Gonige/Gnige (av): At least/at all

Googseke (vai): S/he is hunting frogs

Goojin (vai): S/he is hanging

Gookookoo (na): Owl

Gookshki'ewzi (vai): S/he has the ability to

Goon (na): Snow

Goonkaa (vii): There is snow on the ground

Gotaan/Gtaan (vti): S/he is afraid of it

Gshkapjigan(an) (ni): Parcel(s)/
package(s)

Gshkitoon (vti): S/he is able to do it

Gsinaamigad (vii): It cold (weather)

Gtaakmise (vii): It is caving in

Gtaamgo- (pv): Expend great effort

Gtaamgozi (vai): S/he is fierce/
formidable

Gtaamgwad (vii): It is storming

Gtaamgwatoo (vai): S/he is fierce/
formidable

Gtaamgwiinmoog (vaip): They are
many/a lot

Gtige (vai): S/he is planting/gardening

Gwaakdaza (vai): S/he is skinny

Gwaansikmii (vai): S/he took off
quickly

Gwech (av): Generally/typically

Gwegwendig (pr-an): Whoever

Gwekaabwi (vai): S/he is turning
around (standing)

Gwetaanse (vai): S/he is walking fast

Gwiidibiwin(an) (ni): Chair(s)

Gwiishkshimaa (vta): S/he is whistling
at him/her

Gwiiwnan (ni): Clothes

Gwiiwzens (na): Boy

Gwiiwzenswi (vai): He is a boy

Gyakse (vai): S/he is walking in right
direction/well

Gyakwan (vii): It is good

Gyakwenmaa (vta): S/he is pleasing
him/her

Gzhaa'aa (vta): S/he is babysitting
someone

Gzhaadaawsa (vai): S/he babysits

Gzhe-mnidoo (na): God/Creator

Gzhide (vii): It is hot

Iidig (av): Apparently/might be/must
be

Iw (pr-in): That (inanimate object)

Jaagdaawe (vai): S/he is sold out of
selling something

Jejenj- (pv): Fancy

Jejenji'ii(n) (ni): Fancy thing(s)

Ji- (pv): Will/shall

Jibwaa (cj): Before

Jiibegamik (ni): Cemetery/graveyard

Jiigbiig/Jiigbiing (av): At the beach/on
the shore

Jiigi- (pn): near

Jiimaan(an) (ni): Boat(s)/canoe(s)

Jiisens(an) (ni): Carrot(s)

Jiiwegaanh (ni): A person's name on
Bkejwanong

Kaakan (ni): Chest

Kagwag (na): Geese

Kawe (av): First of all/first in sequence

Ki (ni): Land/earth/ground

Kida (vai): S/he says

Kina (qnt): All

Kiwenziinh (na): Old man

Kizhebaawgak (av): Morning

Ko (av): Generally/habitually/use to

Ko- (pv): Since/as far as/as long as

Kognaa (vta): S/he was raised/brought
up

Kondiins(an) (ni): Basket handle(s)

Koozi (vai): S/he is a certain height/
length

Kowaabjige (vai): S/he is watching/
standing guard

Kwaandwe (vai): S/he is climbing

Kwe(wag) (na): Woman (Women)

Kwedwe (vai): S/he is asking

Kwejdiwag (vaip): They are asking each
other

Kweji- (pv): Try to do something

Kwejimaa (vta): S/he is asking him/her

Kwejmigaaza (vai): S/he is being asked

Kwejtoon (vti): S/he is trying/testing it

Kwezens(ag) (na): Girl(s)

Maa (av): Here/there

Maaba (pr-an): This (animate)

Maagnige (vai): S/he is weaving
(basket)

Maajaa (vai): S/he is leaving

Maajiigin (vii): It is growing/starting
to grow

Maamiiktawaa (vta): S/he is amazed at
what (another person) says

Maamiikwaabdaan (vti): S/he is
amazed at seeing something

Maamiikwaabi (vai): S/he sees
something surprising

Maamiikwendam (vai): S/he is happy

Maamkaadendam (vai): S/he is
surprised/amazed

Maamkaaztowaa (vta): S/he is amazed
at what s/he says

Maampii (av): Here

Maanda (pr-in): This (inanimate)

Maandaawnaagozi (vai): S/he looks
amazing/really good

Maapiich (av): Eventually/after a while

Maawndoon (vti): S/he is gathering it

Maawnidiwag (vaip): They are
gathering/meeting

Maawnji- (pv): Together

Maawnjidiwag (vaip): They are
gathering/meeting

Maawnjitoon (vti): S/he is collecting it

Madwewebidoon (vti): S/he is shaking
it/moving it around

Magakiins(ag) (na): Little frogs

Ma'iingan (na): Wolf

Makaan/Mkaan (vti): S/he is finding it

Manj (pt): However/wonder how

Mbe (av): Immediately/now

Mbegish naa (ij): Hope that ...

Mbwaach'aa (vta): S/he is visiting him/
her

Mbwaachigaaza (vai): S/he is visited

Mbwaachwe (vai): S/he is visiting

Mchaa(noon) (vii): It is big/they are big

Mdaaswi (nm): Ten

Medewaadzijig (na): Midewiwin
people

Megwaa (av): While/right now

Mekdekonyed (na): Priest/dressed in
black

Memdige (av): Especially

Memkaach (av): Necessary/must/
bother oneself with

Mena (av): All over

Mewnzha (av): Long time ago

Mgoshkaajtaa (vai): S/he is annoying/
disruptive

Midida/Mdida (vai): S/he is big

Migizi (na): Eagle

Mii (av): (That's) when/how/who/etc.

...

Miigaazo (vai): S/he is fighting

Miigaazo-nini (na): Warrior/fighter (male)

Miigaazo-niniikwe (na): Warrior/ fighter (female)

Miijim (ni): Food

Miijin (vti): S/he is eating it

Miikaans (ni): Trail

Miikan (ni): Road

Miikanaake (vai): S/he is making trails/ roads

Miinaa (vta): S/he is giving it to him/ her

Miindiza (vai): S/he is giving up him/ herself

Miinwaa/Miin'aa (av): And/also

Miishkokoong (av): In the grass/on the grass

Miizhgaaza (vai): S/he is given something

Mikwendaan (vti): S/he remembers it/ thinks of it

Minik (av): So much/so many

Minwaanzo (vai): S/he is a nice color

Mishoo/Nmishoomis (na): My grandfather

Mji- (pv): Bad/evil/naughty

Mji-giizhwewin (ni): Swear words/ profanity

Mjikaans(an) (ni): Little fence(s)

Mjikan(an) (ni): Fence(s)

Mkade- (pn): Black

Mkadeke (vai): S/he is fasting

Mkadewaanza (vai): S/he is colored black

Mkadewnaagzi (vai): S/he looks black

Mkadewzi (vai): S/he is black

Mkawaa (vta): S/he found him/her

Mko (na): Bear

Mkowaazhmaa (vta): S/he is reminding him/her

Mkozhwe (vai): S/he is swimming (fish)

Mmaangninjii (vai): S/he has big hands

Mmigwebnaan (vti): S/he is shaking it

Mna-/Mno- (pv): Good/well/pleasant

Mna-bmaadzi (vai): S/he is living well

Mnachge (vai): S/he is doing well/ doing good

Mnapgozi (vai): It (animate) tastes good

Mnataagod (vii): It sounds good

Mnataagzi (vai): S/he sounds good

Mngadeyaa(noon) (vii): It is wide/They are wide

Mnidoo(g) (na): Spirit(s)

Mnidoosh(ag) (na): Bug(s)

Mnikwen (vti): S/he is drinking it

Mnikwewin (ni): Drink

Mnishenh (ni): Island

Mnjimendaan (vti): S/he remembers it

Mnjiminaan (vti): S/he is holding onto it

Mnookmi (vii): It is spring

Mno-yaa (vai): S/he is well (in living)

Moozh'aa (vta): S/he senses him/her presence

Mshkawziimigad (vii): It is strong

Mshkiki (ni): Medicine

Mshkonakii (vai): S/he is a strong worker

Mshkozii (vai): S/he is strong

Mshkoziimigad (vii): It is strong

Mskozi (vai): S/he is red

Mskwaa (vii): It is read

Mtig(oog)/Mitig (na): Tree(s)

Mtigwaaki (ni): Forest/woodland

Mwi (vai): S/he is crying

Mzhwe (na): Cottontail rabbit

Mzinigan(an) (ni): Paper(s)/book(s)

Mzinigani- (pv): Papered something

Na'aa (na): What's his/her name? (expression)

Naa (pt): Emphatic marker

Naa (vta): S/he tells him/her something

Naabi (vai): S/he looks in a certain direction

Naabjitoon (vti): S/he uses it a certain way

Naabwaa (vta): S/he is hooking him/her (fish)

Naadmaage (vai): S/he is helping

Naadmowaa (vta): S/he is helping him/her

Naagzhige (vai): S/he is scraping splints (basket)

Naajmo (vai): S/he tells a story a certain way

Naaknigegamig (ni): Band office

Naakod (vii): It is sticklike

Naakshi (av): It is evening

Naama'iing (av): Underneath

Naan'gidoon (vai): S/he is talking on a certain topic

Naan'godnong (av): Sometimes/occasionally

Naanaagdawendaan (vti): S/he looking after it

Naanan (nm): Five

Naaniibwi (vai): S/he is standing

Naanza (vai): S/he/it animate is a certain color

Naasanaa (av): Be careful/Look out

Naashkowaa (vta): S/he is approaching him/her

Naazh (av): Until/extended period of time

Naazhse (vii): It is sinking down

Nakii (vai): S/he is working

Nakiimigad (vii): It works

Nakmigzi (vai): S/he does certain things

Nam'aa (vai): S/he is praying/Christian

Nam'aawin (ni): Prayer/Christianity

Namoo (vii): It leads a certain way (path/road)

Nanda (pr-in): These (inanimate)

Nankii (vai): S/he is working on it

Nawaj (av): Various

Nbaa (vai): S/he is sleeping

Nbiish (ni): Water

Nbo (vai): S/he is dying/died/passing away

Nbwaakaawin (ni): Wisdom

Nchiiwaa (vta): S/he is scolding him/her

Nchiiwchigaaza (vai): S/he is being scolded

Ndaadzi (vai): S/he is born

Ndabiibiinsim (na): My baby

Ndamaa (vta): S/he is calling out for him/her

Ndamoojge (vai): S/he is fishing

Ndawaach (av): Might as well/instead

Ndawemaa (na): My sibling (opposite sex)

Ndawendaan (vti): S/he wants something

Ndawenmaan (vta): S/he wants someone

Ndose (vai): S/he walks from a certain place

Ndowaabi (vai): S/he is watching for things

Ndowaabmaa (vta): S/he is looking for him/her

Ndowendaan (vti): S/he needs/wants it

Ndowenjgaaza (vai): S/he is needed/wanted

Nendaan (vti): S/he is thinking of it

Nendam (vai): S/he is thinking/deciding

Nengaach (av): Gently/without much force

Neniizh (nm): Both/two each

Nese (vai): S/he is breathing

Nesewin (ni): Breath

Neyaaptoon (vti): S/he puts something back

Ngama (vai): S/he is singing

Ngamwin (ni): Song

Ngashi (na): My mother

Ngitziimag (na): My parents

Ngiza (vai): It (animate) is melting

Ngoding (av): Once

Ngodooshkin (av): A bagful

Ngogaaza (vai): S/he is buried

Ngoji (av): Somewhere/anywhere

Ngonaagzi (vai): S/he disappeared

Ngwaankwad (vai): It is cloudy

Ngwis (na): My son

Ni- (pv): Do something going away/time

Ni'ii (ni): Whatchamacallit

Ni'iing (ni): Whatchamacallit (location)

Nigaa'aa (vta): S/he is mean to him/her

Nigaazi (vai): S/he is poor

Niibaadbik (av): All night long

Niibaaptoo (vai): S/he is running around all night

Niibiish (ni): Leaf

Niibiishaaboo (ni): Tea

Niibna (qnt): Lots/many/much

Niigaan (av): Ahead/in front/in the future

Niigaanii (vai): S/he is in front/in the lead

Niigaanzi (vai): S/he is in charge

Niijaanis (na): My child

Niijkiwem (na): My brother/my friend

Niimidiwag (vaip): They are dancing together

Niin (pr-an): Me/I

Niinaa (ij): "Well"

Niinwi (pr-an): Us (exclusive)

Niiwaak (nm): Four hundred

Niiwin (nm): Four

Niizh (nm): Two

Niizhing (nm): Twice/two times

Niizhwaaswi (nm): Seven

Nike'iing (av): In a certain way/
  direction
Nikeyaa (av): A certain way/direction
Nikoniye (vai): S/he is dressed a certain
  way
Nimaamaa (na): My mother
Nimkiikaa(migad) (vii): It is
  thundering
Nimkii-wiiwkwedong (ni): Thunder
  Bay, Ontario
Nimosh(ag) (na): Dog(s)
Ninaabe (na): My male/husband
Ninda (pr-in): These (inanimate)
Ningbiginwenh (na): Screech owl
Nini/Ninwag (pr-an): Man/men
Ninimod (vii): It leads a certain
  direction (path)
Ninj(iin) (ni): Hand(s)
Nishaa (av): In jest/joking/for nothing
Nishkaadzi (vai): S/he is angry/mad
Nishnaabe (na): Ojibwe person
Nishnaabema (vai): S/he speaks
  Ojibwe
Nishnaabemtowaa (vta): S/he is
  speaking Ojibwe to him/her
Nishnaabemwin (ni): Ojibwe language
Nishnaabens(ag) (na): Little Ojibwe
  people/child(ren)
Niw (pr-ni): Those (inanimate)
Nji (pt): Because of/from
Njibaa (vai): S/he is from a certain place
Njiknaa (vta): S/he is leaving him/her
  behind
Njikse (vai): S/he is appearing walking
Nkweshkwaa (vta): S/he is meeting
  him/her

Nkwetaage (vai): S/he is answering
Nmadbi (vai): S/he is sitting
Nmadbise (vai): S/he falls into a sitting
  position
Nnangbiza (vai): S/he is shaking/
  trembling
Nokii/nakii (vai): S/he is working
Noodin (vii): It is windy
Nooj (av): Various
Noojgaaza (vai): S/he is hired (for
  working)
Nookminensing (av): In the little bush
Nookming (av): In the bush/inland
Nookmis (na): My grandmother
Nookshkaa (vai): S/he is coming to a
  stop/is stopping
Noondaage (vai): S/he hears certain
  things
Noondaagzi (vai): S/he is shouting/
  yelling/calling out
Noondaan (vti): S/he hears it
Noondwaa (vta): S/he hears him/her
Noongwa (av): Today/now
Noos (na): My father
Nootwaa (vta): Repeat what s/he says
Noozwin (ni): Name
Nsaa (vta): S/he is killing him/her
Nsaakbidoon (vti): S/he is opening it
  (pulling it open)
Nsaaknaan (vti): S/he is opening it
Nshiimenh (na): My younger sibling
Nshkaadziitaadoog (vaip): They are
  angry with one another
Nshkaadziitowaa (vta): S/he is angry at
  him/her
Nshkaaji- (pv): Angerly

Nsiwag (vaip): There are three of them

Nswi (nm): Three

Ntaa- (pv): Be good at something

Ntaagod (vii): It is haunted

Ntaasi(wag) (na): Glass(es)

Nwanj (av): More (than something else)

Nwe (vai): S/he speaks a certain way/ sound

Nwemaa (vta): S/he is related to him/ her

Nwewin (ni): Sound/language

Nwezh (av): Long time

Nwiijkiwemag (na): My brothers/ friends

Nzigos (na): My aunt

Oodetoo (vai): S/he is going around shopping

Oodi/idi (av): Over there

Oosan (na): His/her father

Ow (pr-an): That (animate)

Owedi (av): Over there

Paa- (pv): To go around doing a certain thing

Pagdoon (vti): S/he is throwing it

Pagnaa (vta): S/he is throwing him/her/ it (animate)

Pa'iins(ag) (na): Little person(s)/ legendary people

Pane (av): Always

Pichi (na): Robin (bird)

Pii (av): When (at a certain time)

Piichi- (pv): To a certain degree

Piiskaa (vai): S/he walks a certain speed

Piitnakii (vai): S/he worked so much

Piitnokii (vai): S/he worked so much

Pin(iig) (na): Potato(es)

Pipiichin (av): From time to time

Piza (vai): S/he is driving/flying to a certain place

Pshizhe'aa (vta): S/he is strapping/ spanking him/her

Sa (pt): emphatic marker

Saa (vta): S/he is putting him/her in a certain place

Sabaabiins (ni): String/rope

San'goo (na): Squirrel

Sayenh (na): Older brother

Semaa (na): Tobacco

Shaagnaash(ag) (na): White person (people)

Shaagnaashii- (pv): English way

Shaagnaashiikiing (av): On white person's land/world

Shaagnaashiiwinikaade (vii): What it is called in English

Shaagnaashiiwnikaaza (vai): What s/ he is called in English

Shaangshin (vai): S/he is lying around

Shaashaagmaa (vta): S/he is chewing on it (animate)

Shkiniikwe (na): Young woman

Shkiniikwewish (vai): Bad/naughty young woman

Shkinwewi (vai): He is a young man

Shko (dash go) (pt): Emphatic marker

Shkode-naapkowaan (ni): Steamboat

Shkonjgaaza (vai): S/he is left behind

Shkose (vii): It is leftover

Shkwaa- (pv): Finishing/quitting

Shkwaach (av): Last (in a sequence)

Shkwaandem(an) (ni): Door(s)

Shkwe'iing (av): At the end

Shkweyaang (av): Behind/at the end

Shpaawngisin (vii): It is up as a mound

Shpide-dbik (av): Late at night/deep into the night

Shpiming (av): Up high/upstairs/heaven

Shwii (Dash wii) (av): But

Sijgaaza (vai): S/he is put (somewhere/there)

Sko (sa ko) (pt): Emphatic marker

Swii (sa wii) (av): But

Te (vii): To be (in a certain place)

Temigad (vii): To be (in a certain place)

Tikwaans(an) (ni): Small branch

Tiswaa (vta): S/he is dyeing him/her/it (animate)

Toon (vti): To put in a certain place

Wa- (pv): Go and do a certain thing

Wa (pr-an): That (animate)

Waabang (av): Tomorrow

Waabdaan (vti): S/he sees it

Waabdawin (ni): Vision/a thing shown

Waabganoojiinaang (ni): Wallaceburg, Ontario

Waabmaa (vta): S/he sees him/her

Waabndowe (vai): S/he exhibits things

Waabnjigaaza (vai): S/he is seen/they see him/her

Waabnjige (vai): S/he is seeing/watching

Waabshkaankwod (ni): A name on Bkejwanong

Waabshkokiing (ni): Marsh

Waagjiitaa (vai): S/he is bending over

Waasa (av): Far/far away

Waawaach (av): Even (indicating surprise)

Waawaashkesh (na): Deer

Waawiisgagnaamaa (vta): S/he hurts him/her continuously (hitting)

Waawye- (pv): Round

Waawyejiwang (ni): Detroit/Lake St. Clair

Webi- (pv): Begin/start to do something

Webtaa (vai): S/he is starting (to do something)

Wenda (av): Very/completely

Wene (pr-an): Who (in questions)

Wenesh (pr-an): Who (in questions)

Wenjda (av): Very/completely

Wepjigaans(an) (ni): Hammer(s)

Wesiinh (na): Animal

Weweni (av): Carefully/properly/well

Wewiib (av): Hurry/quickly

Wewiibendam (vai): S/he is impatient/overeager

Widi (av): Over there

Wiiba (av): Soon/early

Wiidge (vai): S/he is married

Wiigwaam (ni): Building/house

Wiigwaamens (ni): Little building/washroom

Wiijiiwaa (vta): S/he is accompanying him/her

Wiikaa (av): Ever/late/rarely

Wiindmaage (vai): S/he tells/reports

Wiindmowaa (vta): S/he is telling him/her something

Wiingashk (ni): Sweetgrass

Wiintam (av): His/her turn

Wiisgaak (na): Black ash tree

Wiisgagnaamaa (vta): S/he is hurting him/her by hitting

Wiisginezi (vai): S/he is in pain (physical)

Wiisini (vai): S/he is eating

Wiiwan (na): His/her wife

Wnishin (vai): S/he is lost

Wnishmaa (vta): S/he is making him/her lost

Wnitoon (vti): S/he lost it (something)

Wo-/Oo- (pv): Go and do something

Wodi (av): Over there

Ya'aa(g)/ayaa (pt): What's his name?

Yaa (vai): S/he is (at a location)

Yaa(migad) (vii): It is (at a location)

Yaawaa (vta): S/he has someone/it (animate)

Yekzi (vai): S/he is tired

Zaagdoode (vai): S/he is crawling out of something

Zaag'mo (vii): It is opening/clearing (trails/land)

Zaagwewemaa (vta): S/he is calling out for him/her

Zaajibza (vai): S/he is flying out (of something)

Zaam (cj): Because

Zaam (av): Excessively

Zaasaakwe (vai): S/he hollering/whooping

Zaasgokwaanaa (vta): S/he is frying (animals)

Zanagad (vii): It is difficult

Zeg'aa (vta): S/he is scaring him/her

Zegzi (vai): S/he is scared

Zenbaanh (na): Ribbon

Zhaa (vai): S/he is going to a certain place

Zhaagnaashag (na): White people

Zhaagnaashiimowin (ni): English language

Zhaawanong (av): In the south/to the south

Zhaazhi (av): Already/long time ago

Zhashkoonh (na): Muskrat

Zhawenmaa (vta): S/he blesses/loves him/her

Zhebii'aan(an) (ni): Oar(s)

Zhi- (pv): Certain thing/how

Zhiishiib(ag) (na): Duck(s)

Zhiitaa (vai): S/he is getting ready

Zhimaagaanh (na): Soldier

Zhimaagaawi (vai): S/he is a soldier

Zhinaagod (vii): It looks a certain way

Zhinaagzi (vai): S/he looks a certain way

Zhinaashkowaa (vta): S/he is sending him/her to a certain place

Zhinaazhkaajgaaza (vai): S/he is sent somewhere

Zhinkaadaan (vti): S/he calls it a certain name

Zhinkaademigad (vii): It is called a certain name

Zhinkaanaa (vta): S/he names/calls
him/her

Zhinkaandiza (vai): S/he is calling
himself/herself (name)

Zhinkaaza/Zhinkaazo (vai): S/he is
called (name)

Zhinooge (vai): S/he is pointing

Zhishenh (na): Uncle

Zhitoon (vti): S/he is making it

Zhitwaa (vta): S/he is making it for
him/her

Zhiwdoon (vti): S/he is taking it to a
certain place

Zhiwebad (vii): It is happening

Zhiwebizi (vai): Something happen to
someone

Zhiwnaa (vta): S/he is taking someone
to a certain place

Zhiyaa (vai): S/he feels a certain way

Zhiyaa(migad) (vii): It feels a certain
way

Zhiyaawngide (vii): Something
unexpected happen

Zhizhyaaw (av): Straight

Zhoonyaa (ni): Money

Zhoonyaake (vai): S/he is making
money

Zhoonyaakenswi (vai): S/he is making
a little bit of money

Zhoonyaans (ni): Little bit of money

Zhooshmiingweni (vai): S/he is smiling

Ziibi (ni): River

Ziibiins(an) (ni): Creek(s)

Ziigwebnaa (vta): S/he is spilling it
(animate)

Znagad (vii): It is difficult

Znagzi (vai): S/he is difficult

About the Contributors

Mkadebineshii-kwe, Jennie Blackbird, was born and raised on Bkejwanong. She is a residential school survivor and has been assisting with language revitalization for over twenty-five years. She has also helped with the *Nishnaabemwin Online Dictionary*.

Bemgiizhgookwe, Joanne Day, was born and raised on Bkejwanong. She is a residential school survivor and has been helping with language revitalization for over twenty years. She is the sister of Doopinibiikwe. She has also helped with the *Nishnaabemwin Online Dictionary*.

Doopinibiikwe, Linda George, was born and raised on Bkejwanong. She is a residential school survivor and has been assisting with language revitalization for over twenty years. She is the sister of Bemgiizhgookwe. She has also helped with the *Nishnaabemwin Online Dictionary*.

Noodin, Eric Isaac, was born and raised on Bkejwanong. He is a residential school survivor and is a traditional Anishinaabe knowledge holder who has been helping with language, culture, and ceremonial revitalization and teachings.

Naawkwe-giizhgo-kwe, Reta Sands, was born and raised on Bkejwanong. She is a residential school survivor and has been assisting with language revitalization for over forty years. She has also helped with the *Eastern Ojibwa-Chippewa-Ottawa Dictionary* and *Nishnaabemwin Online Dictionary*.

Kaangaadese, Edwin Taylor, is a second-generation residential school survivor. He is an avid learner of Anishinaabemowin and has been teaching and sharing language songs for over fifteen years.

Mkoons, Ira White Sr., was born and raised on Bkejwanong. He is a residential school survivor and has been helping with language revitalization for over fifteen years. He has also helped with the *Nishnaabemwin Online Dictionary*.